The Faded *Flower*

The Faded *Flower*

DERRICK HARDING

ISBN: 978-621-434-061-3 (softcover)
978-621-434-062-0 (hardcover)

Printed in New York by:

OB | OMNIBOOK Co.

OMNIBOOK CO.
99 Wall Street, Suite 118
New York, NY 10005
USA
+1 202-738-1322
www.omnibookcompany.com

First Edition

For e-book purchase: Kindle on Amazon, Barnes and Noble
Book purchase: Amazon.com, Barnes & Noble,
and www.omnibookcompany.com

Omnibook titles may be purchased in bulk for educational, business, fund-raising, or sales promotional use.
For more information please e-mail info@omnibookcompany.com

Design by: Gian Carlo C. Tan

Contents

Chapter 1

Lily Smith Abigail Parks was the pride and joy of Zelda and Jeremiah Parks, an offspring conceived out of desperation and birthed from tragedy. Yet, she didn't allow her past circumstances to overshadow her future. She was a tall stately honey brown skin lady with a lean and beautiful frame. She distinguished herself in a crowed by her natural height and Nigerian's colourful head band. She took pride in her natural braided hair and always wore this colourful headband to keep them in place. She has struggled against factions, defied many odds and rose to stardom, to, fulfill her mother's now- functional dream. She wouldn't allow it to die. Faded yes, but not dead, and causes her to reflect on Dreams Deferred by Langston Hughes. What happens to a dream deferred? He asked

Does it dry up,
Like a raisin in the sun?
Or fester like a sore--
And then run?

Does it stink like rotten meat?
Or crust and sugar over--like a syrupy sweet?
Maybe it just sags like a heavy load.
Or does it explode?

Lily's dream didn't fester, stink, sugar crust or explode but she rose triumphantly from nothingness, to stardom.

Her mother Zelda Elizabeth Parks, affectionately called Zell, was 45 years old on that special day twenty -two years ago, but she looked more like 21years old. She leaned with discomfort against their prized soup- up black four door 1965 Morris Oxford motor car. She rested the flat palm of her left hand protectively on her protruding stomach. The effects of her seven-month pregnancy, heightened her cool dark complexion with a healthy glow. She was completely engrossed in thoughts about their heir of promise. And, although she displayed seaming discomfort, she looked beautiful in the pleasant afternoon sun. In fact, her spotless radiance revealed an intricate and refined delicacy that distinguished her ladylike qualities. Every hasty man would wish that their wives were always pregnant to preserve such exquisite charm.

With quick fluid movement, she switched her dark curly hair, like a black silken scarf, from the left side of her head to the right. Her hair was drawn back smoothly, revealing her lovely oval shaped face with high cheek bones, thick negroid lips and graceful curvy neck. Her hair was tied and dangled in a mane that hung down her back. Her five feet three-inches frame was distorted only by her posture against the car that supported her in the uneasiness she felt after standing for some time. Yet, what was so unusual about this little diamond, was not just that she was such a stunningly, beautiful unassuming lady, that every level-headed man would rival for her; nor because the foolish in their drunken stupor, would declare that they would swim the broadest river or climb the highest mountain to get to her, but, because she was consumed by an acute passion. Hers' was the pride of womanhood. It was the anticipated gift of arduous toil. It was the joy that set every mother apart, who cherished the growth of a human being kicking inside their womb. It was this burning desire to bear her first child, that gave her hope. In fact, this child was her panacea. This was the real proof that after every tragedy in one's life, one must still hope

"Hope, as Alexander Pope says
It springs eternal in the human breast;
Man, never Is, but always to be blest.
The soul, uneasy, and confined from home,
Rests and assured in a life to come."

She like many others in adverse situation, find comfort in hoping. Zell's purpose was clear. Whatever the circumstance, regardless how impossible it may seem. So, there is never in her situation, a dark cloud, without a silver lining. "Her weeping might have endured for a night, but joy came in the morning." She like many in her predicament believed and thought optimistically that something better was in their future.

The radiance that glowed on her face after all her misfortunes, was the unspoken evidence that she was prepared not to go down without a fight. So, she stood the test of time for ten years. Some smart aleck would say, you waited long time, so you can, still wait a little bit longer. Yet, pardon me, let the human in her vent. Let it bubble. Let it erupt and flow like a Hephaestus lava. Let her thoughts flow, slithering slow and consuming every negative thought that stand in her way. Rise lady. Confirm your hurt. Yet silently, she bottled them. She bottled them, and they fermented as the Douro Red Casual Garcia wine that Jerry surprised her with on one of her birthdays. She waited anxiously some more, for Jerry. He was scheduled to take her to the hospital where she would spend the next two months on her back until she delivered her salvation. She became exhausted and she began to raise questions. She gesticulated, she whispered her disgust, she threw her hands in the air and went back into the car to wait. She waited, because psychologically and emotionally, she was trapped in her cocoon of modesty. How could she, when the butterfly should demand wings to fly, yet she held her peace, and sang "Blessed assurance Jesus is mine." She never expected this from Jerry.

"Coming Zell, coming dear," the careless king apologized, so with this sugar-coated band- aid he encouraged her. He revealed solemn anxious copper-brown face, sympathetic eyes and a rather tall angular head. He stood about six feet five inches on strong brawny limbs. He was her king alright, husband and friend and she was very proud to be carrying his child. So, she submitted to him. He turned his body full twist. His boots trampled ruinously on the wet grass and soft clay as his forgetful act, crushed the sweet spirit of the silent sufferer.

He stood astride a concrete, rectangular cistern. His legs firmly planted, his back arched as his hands squelched a spectrum of multi-coloured, rainbow, soapy water glistening in the sunlight. "Coming Zell, coming sweetie." He washed and strained his neck to glance around at her. "You have waited long enough." However, she was 'fermenting,' too infuriated to respond, she only frowned. He rushed toward the house, wiping his wet hand on his polka dot – greenish banana stained khaki pants. He kicked off his boots. He stepped across the veranda sudden splashing of water confirmed his lateness and urgency. His voice shouting above the sound of the water, proclaimed his enjoyment yet, didn't differ time, the ticking of the clock continued.

'How great thou art, how great thou art," he sang to an elaborate crescendo. Suddenly, the splashing stopped. The singing simmered to a hum. Then in one quick as a blink motion he tried to make up for lost time. The agile forty-two-year-old athletic figure bustled toward his 'damsel' in distress, kicking stones, buckling his belt, then rolling up his shirt sleeves. Zell was by then totally exasperated. She was seething hot, boiling with impatience. The new old Morris Oxford couldn't offer comfort. The darling Sweet-pet had no air condition. If the passenger's seat could talk it would complain and make things easier for her. Jerry approached her. He wasted little time in igniting the dependable machine.

And as it were, pampering the engine, he called her by name "Come now Sweet pet." He turned the key once. "Now don't let me down," He coaxed the engine. He tried a second time. H-um- hum- hum the she roared the most pleasing sound to the driver's ear. See, "I know it. This is a faithful girl." And Zell. Retorted inwardly: from her ambience of fear. "Faithful car, faithful man!" "O she never lets me down." Sweet-pet spattered and zoomed loudly. Puffs of grey smoke gushed from her exhaust pipe and raked up dust like an Ego trash blower.

Then, deliberately, according to the manufacturer's script for first gear performance, Sweet-pet concurred, and conquered the rugged. She rocked, as Jerry revved her engine. Up, and up she climbed, until she triumphed at the top of the hill on the bumpy roadway. Her response was unlike any other Jerry heard. She hummed a pleasing melody in first gear, much to the delight of his ears.

"O Sweet-pet," he romanticized her. By then Zell was exasperated'. Why though, did she restrain herself? Was it peace under duress, or a ticking time bomb ready to explode.

Jerry, obviously quite elated about the performance of the car, didn't read her silence. He was oblivious of the silent storm he had created. "Zell we are going to make it this time girl. Trust me."

"Jerry, stop!" Her voice rasped in his ears with decibels of impatience and rancour. "What took you so long? You know we had to go out. You know what the traffic c situation on the road is at peak hours. You know, you know! She screamed, 'yet you are just coming and treating your car life a second lover," Jerry, what is the matter with you? I am scared. I am scared to death."

Jerry was stunned into silence. It took the voice that raised Lazarus from the dead to summon him to reality. Only some winding sections of the road, the uneven surface and speeding vehicles that demanded his concentration, saved him from seriously immersing himself into the abscess of embarrassment. He struggled to reply. He didn't want to further inflame nor aggravate her feelings. He knew how important this child was to them. He wanted one but to her it was a critical need. "Sorry, sorry Zelda. Sorry dear," his voice trembled. He gulped. "I really was not thinking. I really got held up down the farm today. But you were in such a perfect spirit this morning, what has got into you today? Things have been going so very well over the past few days, so I just can't understand."

She turned her face away to avoid showing her tears. "How do you mean what has got into me Jeremiah Parks? She spoke with trembling voice, down in her throat as she spoke through gathered saliva that bubbled through lips. "You know what the doctor said," she sobbed. "So why take chances?"

"Sorry Zelda Darling," and she knew that he meant it. He glanced at her, though she could not see the compassion in his eyes. He reached out and placed his right hand on her left shoulder. She clasped her left palm on his affectionately and leaned her cheek on them, as she held fast to the glass on the window with her right hand.

"Jerry, I am scared. I am scared to death," she repeated.

O, Darling I know. I am so very sorry. His voice trailed off as tears streamed down his cheek.

Jerry and Zell drove on in the tense atmosphere. A strange silence clung to them like mariners holding on for dear life to broken wreckage. Jerry knew that he had caused them to be late. He struggled to swallow. A lump stuck in his throat. With dexterous fingers and brawny hands, he gripped his steering wheel and carefully negotiated the winding roads and swung to avoid treacherous pot holes and speeding mini- buses. However, he disguised his feelings by the level of confidence he displayed under the trying circumstances.

Indeed, it was a nervous time for both Jerry and Zell. They were very romantic and exciting lovers who established a diligent effort for almost ten years in pursuit of their first child. They were more educated about fertility drugs, aphrodisiac foods and substances than any other couple both near and far around Merton Town. They accessed the services of the best gynecologist, their primary physician could have recommended, and they demonstrated works to match their faith. Yet, they never achieved the full measure of success of bearing a child that survived to show their effort. It was an effort that Zell knew that she had worked for. She closed her eyes and she held firmly to this thought. Then like magic a hymn oozed from deep in her soul:

"When my life's work on earth is ended, and I cross the swelling tide
When the bright and glorious morning I shall see
I shall know my redeemer, when I reach the other side
And His smile shall be the first to welcome me ......"

Oh! She paused as she saw herself being wooed by the Savior's love. She closed her eyes tightly. She drew deep breaths to calm herself. She hugged herself as if she was holding the picture she saw and pressed it close to her heart as possible.

Suddenly, she stopped. A bittersweet experience radiated from the secrets of her mind. It was the death of her last child. Three previous miscarriages reflected no clue to the tragedy of that loss. None of the others was as dangerously honey sweet yet devastating nor dramatic. She buried her head in her palms as she viewed the panoramic view that captured her imagination. She had a most unusual start to that pregnancy, in that she didn't suffer the effects of nauseous reaction that she had at the start of the other pregnancies. It was her birthday and she conceived that night. She smiled at the thought.

That morning, there was no mist to dim the splendor of the sunburst that gave life to the fertile landscape, of the romantic estate of Tumba's valley. The Parks awoke in very high spirits. It was the kind of atmosphere that neither of them wished for even the slightest misunderstanding to interfere with the other's sense of well- being. Hence, they both played a perfect lover's game.

"Zell, the romantic head spinner teased. We are having an emergency session which will involve some ladies at our Jamaica Agriculture Society meeting tonight and I would like you to come."

"You want me to come?" "Of course!" "Jeremiah Parks, what day is today?" "Tuesday April 24th."

"Is that all you can remember, smart guy?"

"You know that I know. I always know; and whom do you think should know better than I, your king and confidant." He took her gently into his arms and kissed her lightly on her forehead; he kissed her neck. He ran his lips down her bosom, then raised his head suddenly and said: "Girl, look at you, I could not ask for a better pair. How could I forget the birthday of the most charming girl to ever come into my life?" Then, she leaned way backward, while he bent so that his outstretched arms supported her at her slender waist.

She flashed her thick, black jerry curls of plaits on her head from one side to the other and looked in his eyes. "How do you expect this beautiful wife like me to spend the prime time of her birthday in a boring old meeting discussing the farmer's dilemma?"

"No-o-o, I am sure that she deserves much more than that, much, much more. Shall I give to her the half of my kingdom, the diamonds on my crown, or a most romantic night under the quizzical gaze of the twinkling star? When the full moon blooms in June without the trace of gloom, and the smell of the cuscus grass come floating toward us and wafting on the breeze; you'll feel your heart dancing merrily to the swishing of the wind in the leaves. Then by the logwood fire we build, we snuggle up near the flickering embers. We could watch the fireflies romancing in the dark and make love wishes under the watchful eyes of the smouldering popping embers." Then, he relaxed his hold of her, and placed a finger on her lip and continued to speak. "Just if we are lucky, we will see a meteorite darting across the sky and make that wish." Om, what will be your wish, my love? Shall it be that your king shall live forever? Shall it be that he be as wise a Solomon, and strong as Samson?" Then he stopped suddenly, and laughed, "I can't be like Samson. I am six feet tall and Samson was a little dude," he said. "That is why his strength created such an impact."

"O Jerry, Mr. Romantic. I will choose to romance under the watchful eyes of the logwood fire. I will settle for your romantic night. And by the way, I would hope that you carry inner strength like Samson, but not be so foolish to tell your secret to Delilah."

He stopped her and placed a finger on her lips again. "You speak too much lady. I will not go that route for all the riches in Palestine." She hugged him. She kissed him, once, twice, and again. "Woops, don't spoil your day, save some for later." He danced around with her, and she gazed into his eyes.

"Let us begin now," she said.

"When lover girl? Now? How can we go out in the open field at this moment?"

"No, I mean here! Right now!" She clung to him.

When the smoke clears, she lay quietly admiring Jerry, the sun was blazing through the bedroom window. Jerry awoke from his doze and remembered that he should have met Dave from 6:00 am, down at the farm.

"Wow! Zell, what time is it?" "Seven fifteen."

"Seven fifteen!" "Oh, my Lord!" He gulped down a cup of coffee, shuffle ed in his amused, she laughed heartily as she called out to him. "Be careful lover boy." She rolled over and clasped her hands over her chest.

Zell was very suspicious when she took out her red dress for the afternoon's occasion. Immediately her heart started dancing. It was quite a fancy evening gown. In her opinion the occasion could best be considered ordinary, yet that was the dress she would wear. She would probably seem over-dressed, but she had the perfect excuse. It was her birthday. She held the dress against her body and scrutinized herself in the mirror, then she practiced a few dance steps, as she hummed the tune: This Magic Moment by Jay and the Americans

When she mentioned wine, she salivated. She could sense the rich red Cruz Garcia Real Sangria gentle trickling down her throat. She coughed at the thought until her eyes were wet with tears.

Though it was customary for her to be escorted out on dates, she felt butterflies in her stomach, from the anticipated surprise that Jerry was so capable of creating. On one of her birthdays she insisted that they should not have an elaborate celebration. They got dressed and simply went for a ride. He drove her slowly and they chatted. But she noticed that he was heading into strange places she had never gone before, only to find out that he had this big bash planned, with a hired band waiting to perform.

And true to form, this night confirmed her suspicion. It was an exotic affair, one of the best she had ever encountered for a long time, perhaps because of the tremendous effort put into transforming the meeting hall and its surroundings, like a hotel ball room. The occasion was not actually a meeting, but a birthday bash put on for some five wives of members of the "J.A.S" branch. The caterers were professionals. They provided excellent music, sumptuous food, and fine wine. Each of the ladies got several presents, and they crowned the evening dancing under the stars.

Zell was elated. They exchanged partners and really danced in the cool night air. Nearing the end, Zell had this tremendous inner urge to be alone with Jerry. She walked away from center stage to the far end of the compound. Jerry took note of the challenge and followed her. It was the kind of urge that every sensitive husband responded to, so as not to spoil a wonderful evening for his partner. She reached out and hugged him tightly and said in a deep sensual voice, "Take me to your castle." It was that voice that was laced with passion, a reaction he never heard since the day of their honeymoon. An avalanche of aphrodisiac memories skidded down the right side of his brain.

Jerry played them distinctly with a feeling of nostalgic aura that danced with pseudo exotic pleasure in the teenager's head when he had his first kiss. Yes, he remembered well that Thursday afternoon. The evening breeze coming from the blue Caribbean Sea was crisp and warm. They arrived at Roland Mill Hotel in Handover with mounting expectation having courted with only the occasional kiss and rare moment of sexual encounter. Time was of the essence. It was 5:30 p.m. The bellhop walked briskly before them to the small cottage with their bags. Jerry tipped him generously and he danced, whistled and leaped into the air as if he was expecting to be snapped in a picture from behind, then he disappeared. Before Jerry could lift her over the threshold she grabbed him, ripped off his shirt exposing the full bloom of his rippling muscles and threw herself in his arms and said, "Take me baby. Take me now." He hugged her and caressed her with passion. These memories still danced in the school boy's mind with a certain admirable charm. Hence, he knew that, that birthday night promised much on its romantic menu. Yet, he wondered if after ten years and after losing four children she could ever press that button of passion and sustain it. They had so many passionate and romantic moments: weekends at fantastic hide-outs, nights at the beach, camping at the river near their home and candle light dinner at home and in fancy restaurants, yet he felt like an anxious teenager.

As he drove from the compound Sweet pet charged like a stallion possessed at the start of a Darby. It was a response of superb efficiency. The tires stirred gravel, leaves, and other flying debris to signal their sudden departure.

A scant five minutes elapsed before they came charging, rocking and bumping down the driveway and into the opened garage. Jerry didn't linger. He locked themselves inside. He dove and shuffled his six feet plus of brawny frame in to the back seat and to his amazement, Zell was sensitive to his touch and he touched the right buttons. His voice quivered and trailed off as he sighed deeply and moaned.

Just after midnight they got dressed and he lifted her to his perfumed bed. "I hope you had a pleasant birthday," he kissed her, and she groaned.

"O dear, this was better than camping under the stars." I didn't see the fireflies, but I saw your passionate eyes. I didn't feel the wind but your warm breath in my ears. Most of all, I didn't see a meteorite darting across the sky. Instead, I saw a happy, smart little girl running to your arms and calling Daddy, Daddy! You lifted her. You hugged her. You spun round and round because she was the joy you waited for. Jerry fell on his knees and they prayed together, and Jesus became the center of their lives.

It was 5:00 P.M. They drove on. Zell closed her eyes as Jerry swerved Sweet Pet over one pothole to the other. How well she remembered the Friday morning after her birthday, it was as crystal clear. She twitched her hands in her lap. She gasped for breath. The radiant sunlight was already agleam through her bedroom window. She went to the window and breathed her pair of forty-five-year-old lungs, full of cool revitalizing air. The bright and beautiful morning confirmed her healthy spirit. She raised her hands in acknowledgment. She inclined her head toward the table in the corner. A tray with a thermos of hot water and goodies for a sandwich and tea was waiting for her. A toaster was plugged in ready, if she needed toast to satiate her apatite. Yet her stomach was filled. She was fully satisfied as if she had just eaten.

Therefore, she pulled out a drawer of soft unworn baby's clothes and cuddled some of them to her chest. She thought that they bore a distinctive smell of a new born infant; and how she craved the feeling of its warm body against hers. With expectant joy in her heart she sought through the clothes and warm blankets with trembling hands. She touched them delicately as she was comforting her child. She lay on the bed and suddenly a feeling of horror came over her.

"No Lord, no Lord, not again." She vividly remembered the death of her child.

She ate very small meals four five times for the day, much to her surprise. She could drink all the fresh milk and ate fruits; without getting nauseous. Hence, she was very positive that, that baby was to fulfill her lifelong dream. Yet, the favourable thoughts were gagged and strangled into silence, as the negatives brazened themselves through her mind. She couldn't brush aside the fright, which possessed her on that unforgettable morning when she fainted and later discovered that she was haemorrhaging. She twisted the wedding ring on her finger. The prayer she prayed for a safe delivery stood out in her mind, to the extent that she spent the last three months on her back in the hospital and saw the fulfillment. Yet most devastatingly, was that the baby lived only five days after an induced labour. She cringed as she watched him on a monitored screen and saw him fight to stay alive as doctors watched in vain. Then he made three faint cries and remained still. Her prayer was answered, she asked for a safe delivery and that she got.

Zell, with her eyes tightly closed, was not only contemplative but also terrified because apart from confiding in her gynecologist, she had kept her dark secret enclosed in her heart. She slapped her forehead several times reprimanding herself. Oh! She screamed loudly because as a teenager her stepfather sexually molested her. She pushed her left knuckle in her mouth and bit on it, when she remembered how her mother forced her to do an abortion to protect her husband, she was so terrified. She grabbed handfuls of hair from her head and tried to pluck them but couldn't. The procedure left her hospitalized for three weeks, not just from the physical trauma but the emotional scars. No court action was taken because she was afraid to testify in court, for fear of reprisals from her parents. Her stepdad was a deacon and a prominent member, of the community. This was gut wrenching to know that her mother allowed her to go through with it. She wondered how cruel she was. She bit her finger until it bled. On seeing the blood, she wept until her eyes were swollen.

She had several counseling sessions with a psychologist, but that didn't help much. She had Sworn to keep all men at a distance, until she met Jerry. He was the perfect friend and father figure she never had. She loved him with an obsession though she was older than she was. Therefore, she strove with all unobtrusive persistence to convert this into bearing him a child, whom she hoped would erase the memories of her past. Indeed, that child would be her salvation. She closed her eyes tight at the very thoughts. As the tension mounted in her head, she held on tightly to the door of the car as Jerry negotiated the corners. Jerry was not a man of the world although he was not a church man which is highly paradoxical. While he believed in God he never thought it was necessary to become a church member.

Jerry had his share of hard times when he was ditched by a lover. He was obsessed with this blonde. He sent her to school and did everything for her, but he could not come to terms with her mother. She claimed that their difference in age would not work out. Yet he persisted until the day of the wedding, only to have the wedding called off, after spending hundreds of dollars. He walked away without looking back. He encouraged himself as he justified the thought that he spent for a cause greater than he was. He learned many lessons that made him a better man and not bitter. Yet, he was almost vain in his thoughts. He was having the time of his life as he remembered the afternoon when the magic of their union started. Thanks to the tremendous hope and confidence that had brought them together.

He was returning from the capital of the second city Manteca Bay, when on reaching Murton Town square, a thunder storm afforded himself and her the rare pleasure of meeting. While they sheltered at the Man-sell Bar and grocery. He lingered over one Red Stripe beers as the rain continued. He wondered how blessed he was to be sitting comfortably, while rain was watering his farm.

A lizard slowly skulked its way in a well-intentioned stroll at the moth gathered around the fluorescent lamp. Thunder grumbled grand and loud overhead and rumbled away into the distance from this serial. The lizard snapped his tongue over and over with deft precision, like lightning slicing through the darkness. Jerry had time and pleasure of amusing himself, as he mused over each catch and the differences in caricatures on the wall of each patron. But, he was jolted back to reality when suddenly the chance of a life time captured his gaze. He gulped a large sip of beer. The dark sun glazed skin angel parted the beaded curtain between the club and the supermarket and wheeled back outside. Jerry thought that he had a dream.

Dream he thought to himself, or probably he was getting drunk, but with one beer? No way. He sat on pins for a few anxious seconds then, he jumped up and pursued the pleasures of his heart. He must have been very persuasive. There must have been an instant surge of high emotion or some strong curiosity that caused the lady to follow him into the club, which she had never done before. Accordingly, for some moments, they sat and stared at each other, occasionally apologizing when their feet deliberately met. The rain lingered. The clock ticked on and they watched the dancers who drank and sang. For the first time in her life, Zell felt comfortable in the presence of the opposite sex, which she marvelled over for many days. Three months passed. Fate did the rest. Zell was named Mrs. Parks.

Chapter 2

Jerry was deep in his fit of nostalgia when suddenly the horn of a speeding truck blasted around from behind.

"Jerry, watch out! Watch the truck, the truck!"

"Hold on Zell, hold on. Excellent, Sweet pet excellent." He dexterously maneuvered the old Morris Oxford around the corner and out of the path of an oncoming Ford van, but not quite out of danger. The rear end of the truck dragged heavily on the right rear end of the car and spun it around. Jerry was powerless to stop the impending fate. The car over turned, rolled over two or three times and flung Zell outside into the path of another vehicle.

In a matter of minutes, the screeching tires, the shouting voices, the crunch of metal and the evidence of flying debris settled but the smell of motor oil, burning rubber and the odour of blood to reveal the ghastly tale of tragedy. Zelda was first to be given attention, because she was making most noise. She bumped heavily against the van and was screaming before she lost consciousness. She was bleeding profusely. Her legs were badly crushed. Her left hand was missing. It was seen twitching on the side of the road. Jerry was trapped in the car saying. "Oh, Sweet pet, girl I failed you today," then he, too, went unconscious. He was pinned behind the steering wheel and a welding torch had to be employed to cut him free.

"You are really one tough cookie old fellow," the torch man said.

Luckily an open-back police vehicle was passing and transported them to the hospital, leaving the ghastly scene of blood and crunched metal behind. Meanwhile, the truck had swerved off the road, fell, and rolled some 10-25 feet below.

Fortunately, the lone driver sustained only a few cuts and bruises when he jumped out and got caught in a tree. The driver of the van got out safely with minor bruises because he was wearing his seat belt. He was so frightened he kept saying, "A say look here! A say look here!" Zell had not been wearing a seat belt because of the pregnancy. The belt caused her much discomfort. The driver of the truck and van were admitted to the emergency ward and treated for shock and minor bruises. They were released a few days after. In the hospital they were visited by the police and members of their insurance company. Jerry was not interfered with until he was released from the hospital. Except for cuts on his face and damage to his shoulder and feet he was alright. He just needed a few sessions of physiotherapy.

"Where am I? Where is Zell? Is Zell- Zell all right?" Jerry responded from his hospital bed two days later. He could smell the scene of the accident.

"Doctor, he has regained consciousness," a voice spoke by way of telephone, "but he is still delirious."

"O my head, Zell! Is Zell alright? Where am I?"

"Please Mr. Parks, take it easy. You have had a very bad accident. Don't get upset again."

"What Accident? Accident, accident, I have an accident." And he laughed loudly. "Jerry had an accident," he sang.

"Yes. You have been unconscious since Friday. Just a moment Mr. Parks."

"Since Friday…," and he slipped away into unconsciousness again. "I am sorry Doctor; he slipped away again. Please continue."

"As I was saying Miss Pine, administer the same medication, give the same dosage."

"Ok, Doctor Roland." She hung up the receiver and prepared to administer the medication, when suddenly he opened his eyes again. "Yes Mr. Parks you came in on Friday afternoon. Come now sir, this is to help you, be good now."

Jerry did not reply to her. "O my head, my head. Is Zell alright?" Likewise, Nurse Pine didn't respond to him but completed the instructions she received. Nurse Pine, Elizabeth Pine as she was known was an RN for ten years. She was married and the mother of three children. She was African American, short and dark skinned. She was medium built and was very swift on her feet. She was reliable and have handled several cases like that of Mr. Parks on several occasions.

He fell asleep almost instantly but woke up about three hours later. This time he was much less sedated. Dr. Roland walked in just in time to witness a faint smile vanishing from his lips as quickly as it came. "Doctor I am glad you have come," he said in a low voice, as he struggled to wave his arms. "You tell me the truth," he sobbed. "Is Zelda alright? Where is she?"

"I tried to explain to him doctor, but...

"Ok Nurse Pine, that will be all for now. The frank middle-aged Causation of European descent stopped her. I will be with Mr. Parks for a little while. See if matron has any dinner to give him. You must be famished," he now turned to Jerry. The nurse left the room and closed the door but lingered outside to listen. Dr. Roland was a tall man, fair blue eyed and straight white hair.

"Yes doctor, I am very hungry, but you have not told me about Zell," he said with an expectant tone. "Is she alright?"

Nurse Pine moved on. "Poor man" she said.

"Well in a matter of speaking, yes, Mr. Parks. She is. What I, well, what I mean is that she is not feeling any pain. I am sorry that we were unable to tell you before. But she hemorrhaged so much that if we had delayed the delivery of the baby to save her life, you would have lost both mother and child. However, you have a very healthy baby girl."

Jerry wept in a long, subdued tone. Dr. Roland picked up his docket, wrote on it, and gave him a good brotherly squeeze on his shoulder.

"Mr. Parks, she died for a cause. Isn't it good to be still alive and to have a beautiful daughter?" He closed the door behind him without waiting for a reply.

Jerry mourned some more. An hour passed before he fell asleep, yet he remained very remorseful. While he fell asleep he dreamt of angels in white carrying Zell away, as she said I will see you someday Jerry. The sound of a daughter certainly brought music to his ears that at first, he could not thoroughly enjoy. But as he gave thought to his circumstances, he hung on to the simple fact that life was not totally hopeless.

At 5:00 pm, Nurse Pine and a member of the kitchen staff entered his room again. "Mr. Parks we have brought you some dinner. We came earlier but you were asleep, so we returned your meal to keep it warm.

Jerry opened his eyes and sat up. He rubbed his eyes. He yawned. He took the tray, nodded but he ate very little and didn't speak. Tears streamed down his face as the nurse and her assistant left without speaking to him again.

They walked some distance down the corridor in silence, then the kitchen assistant spoke "Poor man, he misses his wife." Pine wiped a tear from her eye then she said, "I hope he is not blaming himself. After all, the man still has a beautiful daughter and many years to watch her grow up. Well, she could have died too. All of them could have died," the kitchen assistant added.

Jerry finished his meal and struggled to get out of bed. He stood by the window and stared far away - far beyond the horizon and into his future. He rubbed his chin. He drummed his fingers on the window pane. He swivelled his thoughts round and around in his mind. He looked back at his past and he examined his present condition. Tears filled his eyes, but they were not tearing of remorse this time, but rather mixed reaction. He wished that the future was not so complicated, but he realized that he couldn't escape it. He was confronted by two immutable facts: He was a widower and as a single parent, he held the explicit responsibility of fathering and mothering an innocent child that was his and Zell's greatest desire.

"After all, I am not sure that this matter of trying so hard to have a child was the wisest thing. God knows man's need and satisfies it, how and when He wants to. Every time Zell and I came near to having a child we hit a roadblock, and now this. We have one and Zell is dead." The awesome reality gripped his mind and held it firmly. His heart raced. His eyes felt as if they were rolling over in his head. The whole building was tumbling. He held on to the window ledge but lost all sense of reality. He returned to his surroundings only when he heard Dr. Roland's voice.

"No Mr. Parks don't' say that, you will not fail, we know you will not fail. However, you must be careful not to stand up too long. You could have hurt yourself when you fell." Slowly his eyes opened. The mist passed, and he saw Nurse Pine and Dr. Roland over him. He attempted to rise from his bed, but the doctor restrained him with a gentle hand on his chest.

It was not the first time that he found himself between a rock and a hard place and he drew strength, satisfaction, and peace of mind from praying. He closed his eyes, waited, and then words came. He could not tell what time Dr. Roland and Nurse Pine left, nor could he remember how long he prayed, but when he opened his eyes the next morning and saw the bright and glorious sunlight radiating through his room window, he knew that he must have contacted Him who answered his prayers in the past.

He responded to a world of hope and tranquillity, that he matched with a secured spirit of determination and he didn't hesitate to express his will: "I have never failed in my life, and I'm not about to do so now. I'm a father and I shall be a darn good one." Before he could finish, he remembered Zell. He closed his eyes. He refused to cry. A huge lump stuck in his throat. He groaned, and he sighed. He jammed his hands in his pockets. Instantly he removed them. He slammed his hand against the bed several times, when suddenly a picture of Zell mirrored on his mind impressively. Dressed in white, she was standing at the door holding the baby in her hand and saying, "Jerry, here is Lily."

Joyfully he arose in response to a rap on the door. Then just as he figured, Nurse Pine walked inside holding the baby. Dr. Roland came in after. He moved forward and took the tiny seven -and-a-half pound bundle of life and gazed intently at her. Then with earnest affection he clasped her gently to his chest for an unusual length of time. He closed his eyes tightly until tears trickled down his face. He looked at the child again and was choked by a sudden burst of emotion. Immediately Dr. Roland moved with urgency and rescued the child from his grasp. He handed her to Nurse Pine and laid a comforting hand on Jerry's shoulder.

"You are beautiful little Lily. You are as beautiful as Zell," Jerry said over his shoulder as he went toward his bed.

"Ok Mr. Parks," Dr. Roland said. "You will be able to take Lily home with you this afternoon." He beckoned to Nurse Pine to return Lily to her crib and saw her wiping a tear from her eye. He continued, "There is something I meant to ask you. What are your plans for your daughter? I know you said you would not give her up for adoption but if you wish to speak about the subject I'm here to listen. Would you like me arrange for a social worker to come in and speak to you? Would you like that?"

"I have no thought of giving her up for adoption, but I guess it would do no harm if she came and spoke to me. I'm open to learn as much as I can," Jerry replied.

Jerry watched as they left. The rest of his day was spent in reading the Scriptures and meditating. The words of Jeremiah 1:8 stood out in his thoughts: "Behold, I am with you to deliver you, says the Lord." Indeed, he had found strength in God and a purpose for which to live. The hands of his bedside clock moved slowly. He was already dressed and waiting when Nurse Pine entered through his open door carrying the baby. Jerry reached out eagerly and received

Lily, with father's arms that had divine strength and support. He pictured Zell sitting beside him sharing his joy.

His thoughts were interrupted by a knock on the door. He responded to the knock reluctantly as he was expecting the social worker to visit him, but just hoping she would not come. He invited her in and then sat on the bed, while she sat on the lone chair in the room. She introduced herself as Miss Claudette Evans. She had been a social worker for eleven years. She had several of forms, that were prefilled in and just needed signatures. Jerry focused on the child and refused to look at her. She didn't admire the child, didn't hold her or referred to her as a person. She was strictly for business.

After her introduction and greetings, she said, "Let's get down to business. I understand that you are a single parent now. I am very sorry to hear of the passing of your wife. I understand what you are going through."

"Do you?"

"It must be very hard on you; that is why I've come to see talk, so you can make arrangements to put the baby up for a wonderful life."

"Who says I want to put up my baby for adoption?" He raised his head for the first time. He clasped the baby to his chest. "Who gave you that idea?" Lily started to fuss, and he hushed the baby by patting her back gently.

"Nobody gave me the idea, I am trying to help you. I know how hard it is for you, being a banana farmer and all that. So, I brought all the documents pre-signed. All you have to do is to state your willingness by signing your signature on each document and I will take it from there."

"You know that I am a banana farmer; what else do you know about me? Do you know how hard we tried to have a child? Do you know the depth of the emotion that almost strangle me every time I hear in my mind the crunch of metal, the smell of burning tires? Can you imagine my pain every time this baby cries? But you come in here with your plans to beguile me of the pride of my life."

"No, no! I will find a wonderful wealthy family where your baby will grow up and get the best care possible. I've been in this business a long time and I know how to get the best deal for my patients."

"Well Miss Evans, I never have and never will put up this child for adoption. Therefore, you can take your documents and go back to wherever you came from. Do you know how many years we tried to have a child? I am only sorry Zell is not here to celebrate with me."

The discharged nurse came in and gave him final orders. He received a document which included his information test procedures done, and instructions for administering the medication at home. It also included information for follow up visits and instructions for Physiotherapy treatment. There were also instructions for taking Lily to the clinic.

Soon after, Nurse Pine came in. By then Dave his farm hand also appeared. He took his bags and the quartet left the room where the whiff of his cologne lingered. They proceeded down the corridor as Dave's boots certified their departure, down, down, down the corridor. The door swung and shut again. Nurse Pine exchanged pleasant good byes, and Dave taxied them through the gate and headed for Morton Town.

Jerry returned home to an unexpected welcome organized by Dave before he left to pick him up. Although Jerry was surprised, he never reacted. His entire family of workers on the farm, plus his close neighbours and representatives of the Jamaica Agricultural Society of the local chapter were present. Even Joey his nondescript watchdog was on hand to bark and raced around the yard in a frenzied state.

Jerry stepped out of the truck, holding with esteem pride the beautiful bundle of life, which had become his number one priority. She was cradled in a pink bassinet padded and lined with pink blanket with rectangular pattern in delicate blue colour.

"Here, let me take her for you," a neighbour stepped forward. "Oh, she is beautiful, isn't she a 'Lily'? Jerry stared at her but didn't reply. The folks gathered around to have a closer look at her.

"I am very sorry about Ms. Zelda, Mr. Jerry. I am truly sorry," one member of the farm hands said. "I speak for all of us, right gang?"

"Yes Mr. Jerry we are all sorry," they chimed in unison.

"Thank you all very much. This means a lot to me, to know that you all care. We must pass this way in one way or another at some time. What is important, is how we deal with the pain and suffering, if we can perceive such situations. Most importantly is how our leaving our family and surroundings. Did we leave the situation, a better place and our family better able to cope with life after we have departed this life. This is what you are showing me this afternoon, that in times like these, we all need the support of our friends. Thank you all." Before he was finished his eyes were wet with tears.

Jerry walked to the veranda and sat in his favourite chair. The neighbour who took the baby sat opposite to him where Zelda would have sat. He bowed his head as if he was offering a prayer. Twilight shadows slowly crept into the valley. The last ray of sunlight shone in the topmost branches of the tall June plum tree. The hens clucked and gathered their chickens to their roost and the welcome party drifted up the hill and through the gate. Jerry sat with supreme confidence and silently continued to pray as he waited. The neighbour was about to ask him what his plans were for the night, when a car turned in the driveway and came slowly down.

"Somebody is coming Mr. Jerry."

"I can see that. That seems to be a taxi." "You are right." It was a private taxi, Yet, he bowed his head in acknowledgment.

They both watched as it came rocking down the hill. To his relief...

"Mother am I glad to see you." Jerry rushed from the veranda, took her bag and paid the taxi driver. They hugged each other, as both walked to the veranda.

"Jerry I am very sorry about Zelda. She will be a big loss to you." She exchanged greetings and thanks to Jerry's neighbour, reached down and lifted Lily gently from the bassinet, and kissed her. "Jerry, she resembles you."

"Is that so? I thought she resembled Zell." "That is just sentimental. I know what I see."

The neighbour said goodbye, and Jerry and Lydia relaxed to enjoy the cool air coming up from the valley.

"So, Jerry, what are your plans?"

"Mother, I am just not sure. It is too early to say definitively what I will do."

"You might need to do that fast. I will stay with you for a while. I will certainly do what I can for my granddaughter, but you must think of a long-term solution.

"I am sure I will have to do that mother, but right now I just want to get a good night's sleep. Will you look after her for the night?" Jerry went to his room. He looked around the place. He took up Zelda's photograph and stared at it. He clasped it to his chest and burst in tears.

"Now, now Jerry, come on now, you must be strong. This is what Zelda would have wanted." He rolled over on his stomach and wept himself to sleep.

Lydia sat on the bed beside him, put the bassinet with Lily on a chair, and lay her hand on his shoulders. She was about to dose off when Lily sniffed and sneezed. She jumped up and looked at her. "Bless you." She was fine. She took off Jerry's shoes, covered him with a blanket, then took up Lily and went to the other room.

The next morning Jerry awoke feeling the effects of a hangover as one who partied and drank alcohol all night. Lydia took charge of Lily while he went out to make plans for a memorial service to be held for Zell. While he was out, Lidia fixed herself some breakfast. The funeral service was held a week later at Morton Town Methodist Church where she had her membership, up to the time of her death. The memorial service was not elaborate, though hundreds of people attended. It was very meaningful. Zelda Parks was remembered as a woman who sacrificed her life to achieve her fondest dream. Her body was laid to rest at the eastern corner of the farm below the cassava plot under a large June plum tree, just a stone throw from the river. When Jerry awoke in the mornings and opened his window her tomb was a constant reminder of the beautiful life they both had.

The first few days after the funeral were very hectic for Jerry. The house was strange. Whenever his mother spoke she sounded just like Zell. If the baby cried, he heard sounds as if Zell was comforting her. He quickly recognized his role as that of single parent. But, was ill equipped to deal with it. He took off another two weeks from working on the farm and left Dave to be in charge so that he could adjust more to his fatherly responsibilities. He knew that if Zelda was alive Lily wouldn't lack anything and he wanted to fill that void.

At nights, if Lily cried Jerry and Lydia would-bump heads at the side of the crib. Sometimes both hands hold on to the light switch. When she didn't want to sleep they took turn to hold her. Jerry was sure that everything was under control and he would soon be able to return to the management of the farm.

Unfortunately, things changed dramatically. One night, Lydia received a telephone call, which made her very upset. "Jerry, I have to go home."

"Go home? When?" "Tomorrow!" "Tomorrow?"

"Yes, John is sick, so you have to manage Lily by yourself."

He suddenly felt hopeless and become very angry and was at the verge of tears.

"But Mom, John is a big man," he started to say. "And my husband if you don't realize," she finished.

"How could you leave at this time? I am just getting to understand how to take care of Lily."

"I have had five of you, nobody taught me anything and I managed."

"But mom that was long ago, plus you are a woman. I am a man." "Prove it."

"This is my first child."

"Well, go to the school of hard knocks," she teased. "You have always been on your own and you have survived, and you will now. You have to learn Jerry, you will learn."

Though he was known to be tough and very candid, he was totally surprised at the firmness with which Lydia dealt with the issue. "Mom I am totally disappointed."

"John has been totally disappointed many times, but he sticks with me. You will get over it. I leave tomorrow."

Jerry was overwhelmed and broke down in tears, although he tried, tonight backfired.

"Now, now Jerry you have always been a reasonable man. That is nothing to be disappointed about. You can get a babysitter until I return." She hugged him across his shoulders. H was powerless to stop the tears from flowing.

"I don't want a babysitter, Mother. She is your granddaughter." "But she is your responsibility," Lydia said. "I will give you the names and address of a few babysitters. You may contact them. My husband is sick. I have to go home," she said with an air of finality, and refused to reopen the subject.

Jerry remembered the declaration he made at the hospital. Notwithstanding, he was still shaken by this sudden misfortune. Dave drove his mother to the bus stop the next morning and he was left alone. He was frightened and confused. Lily cried endlessly. He tried every possible thing his limited understanding would allow.

Yet he had no success. He called his mother. Her telephone rang without an answer. He had by then hit the valley of desperation and would have given anything and accepted any solution that would stop Lily from crying. Yet there was one course he could have taken but his pride held him fast in its grip.

"How can I do that? It is almost ten years that we have not communicated."

Yet after trying unsuccessfully to get help, he was left without any other alternative. Jerry had to give up his pride and call her. He paid less attention to her rancour as he remembered that he could catch more flies with honey rather than vinegar.

"May I speak to Daphne?" "This is she. Who is calling?"

"Jerry."

"Jerry?"

"Yes, your brother."

"Jerry my brother! You called me? Are we going to have rain?" "Ok Daphne, let's do the chit chat later. I have a problem."

"You have a problem!" she laughed. "Indeed, you are human after all."

"Daphne, will you stop it?"

"Don't you tell me to stop, ok? I am"

"Lily is crying and will not stop."

"So, check the child's temperature. You have no problem. Only shows my brother is human. Do you have a thermometer?"

"O yes, I believe we have one somewhere, yes." Jerry put down the telephone receiver and reached for the instrument. "I have it here, Daphne."

"Ok, do you know how to use it?"

"Yes, I know how to use a thermometer."

"Now take her temperature." They chatted while he waited on the result. "Alright, how high is her temperature?"

"One hundred and one degrees." "Does she have any cold? 'No' "See? She has a fever. Just get some ice water, put it in her bath tub and immerse her in it for about three minutes." "In the ice water?"

"You'll be surprised. Call me back in another twenty minutes."

Jerry hung up the receiver and followed the instructions. "I am not trying to hurt you Lily, I am not trying to hurt you, but this is what aunty says."

Lily screamed breathlessly.

"Poor baby, Daddy troubles you." He removed her from the water, gave her a quick rub, then gave her a dose of children's Panadol elixir. "Never mind sweetheart." He clasped her to his chest gently. In fifteen minutes the fever was gone but came on and off until it went away altogether. The next morning, he took her to the paediatrician who confirmed that she had a mild upper respiratory infection and recommended treatment.

Chapter 3

After three weeks away from the farm, Jerry realized that he couldn't stay away any longer to take care of Lily. Dave seemed to be managing, but he felt too uneasy. His big problem, however, wasn't just to find a babysitter but a substitute for Zell to mother Lily. He hated the very thought of going back to his mother. John her husband would always be more important. He would always be first choice. Should he become ill or if he needed her to return home. He could have asked Lydia to bring John to his house where she would've access to attend both to he and Lily, but certainly he would never entertain such outrageous consideration. In the past, John was never sympathetic to him or his cause, regardless of how good, interesting or simple it was he would give preference to Daphne. Because she was his choice, Jerry and she were always at loggerheads. Equally, he hated the idea of employing a babysitter. But in the end, he had no choice, and he opted to ask Daphne.

He utilized the list of names and addresses Lydia gave to him. In the period of two weeks Jerry changed three helpers, for one reason or the other. The last one stayed two days. She was totally indignant and frustrated. Her complaint was: "Mr. Jerry was too demanding. The only thing was left for him ask was for me to breast feed Lily." As a result, she didn't even collect her check. Jerry was left with a problem almost as difficult as before. He totally rejected the possibility, of employing another baby sitter. Jerry took on the role of, mother and father so it was time for them to put their heads together and come up with a plan. They fused their hearts and minds and Jerry became the recipient of an active brainstorming process. This resulted in his eliminating one idea after another, until he said, "yes this is it." Jerry was excited. He set out to execute his plan to conquer his fears.

He arranged to temporarily divest the farm to be run by a local banana company, Western Banana Growers. The company would assume full responsibility of the farm on a lease agreement for three years in the first instance but with the option of transferring operations back to him after thirty days' notice, should a problem arise, or he wished to resume his role. His lawyer expedited matters in record time. He was then free to get a steady income and had time to establish himself as mother and father. The missing link in the whole arrangement was that in the true sense of the word, he had been struggling to be a proper parent and this he recognized. He picked up the telephone receiver and dial Daphne's number.

"Hi Daphne."

"Jerry is that you? You never called me back from the night Lily was ill."

"To tell you the truth, this little girl is a handful. She is exactly why I am calling now."

"Really?"

"I have a proposition to offer you. When last have, you taken leave?"

"Not in three years. I was just thinking about taking some; I am tired."

"Perfect! How about coming to rest at my place?"

"What are you up to now Jerry? I am sure you aren't just thinking about my relaxation? Is it Lily again?"

"You are asking too many questions, Sis. Take your leave and you can enjoy a well-earned vacation with Lily." "Of course, you'll enjoy the time. He said"

"Oh Sis, I'll see you next week Thursday a week from today." "Great." At that instance Jerry remembered that he had a session with the chiropractor next day. This experience was enlightening. In fact, he was surprised to learn how simple the treatment was when the doctor explained it to him. He received a pamphlet which supports the doctor's explanation which shows that: Chiropractic is a form of alternative medicine mostly concerned with the diagnosis and treatment of mechanical disorders of the musculoskeletal system, especially the spine. It said that such disorders affect general health via the nervous system. The main chiropractic treatment technique that he used involves manual therapy. He manipulates the spine and doesn't prescribe medication of any form. He would have five sessions with him.

Daphne arrived on Friday afternoon. The weather was quite cold for a tropical day, thanks to the northers: A cold stormy weather coming down from North America. Strange how some people don't enjoy the stormy weather. Yet there is something quite joyful about storms that interrupt routine. In some parts of the world, snow or freezing rain suddenly releases you from expectation and demanding schedules put on you by others. And unlike illness, it is largely a corporate rather than an individual thing. You can just imagine, just still your breathing and listen to the universal sigh. "No work today, no sir." And no one charges you.

Jerry was stuck at home. He was struggling to keep Lily quiet. As usual, when she was uncomfortable, she screamed very loudly as if somebody was hurting her. Daphne was surprised at the strength the child exerted. Her crying was unusually loud.

"Jerry what are you doing to the poor child? Come here sweetheart. Oh, you are wet, oh my." She clasped the screaming child to her bosom. "You are wet dear." She quickly changed her diaper, powdered her and held her close to her and soon she was humming as Daphne rocked her until she was heard no more. She lay her down gently and the peace of sleep comforted her.

Then, for five awkward minutes, silence prevailed. The ticking clock became noticeable. Jerry smacked his tongue over his lips. Daphne stood there and twiddled her thumbs and kept staring at the child. A moth journeyed over the table cloth near the home sweet home lamp and Daphne followed it with her eyes. Jerry seemed embarrassed, yet he knew that he had invited her. Several unanswered questions raced around in his mind and Daphne had her complement as well. He could feel tension building. Something strange was going on in her head but he was not sure if it was annoyance or sympathy. Then courage sprang from the female's heart and she decided that she had enough, since Jerry was unresponsive.

"So, Jerry, how have you been these years? I haven't seen you, heard from you, nor did I care most of the time."

"I, I'm…" Jerry stuttered.

"So, what is this proposal? I know you're not just concerned about me having a good vacation, are you?"

"Yes, no, no, I mean yes. There is a matter which I really wanted to discuss with you."

"What matters? It is Lily, isn't it?" "Where are you going?"

"I'm not going anywhere. Why do you think I'm about to run off and leave her with you? Far from it."

"What I would like you to do is to teach me how to manage her." "You are kidding, right?"

"Dead serious."

"Jerry you're never a mean man. Why don't you employ a babysitter?"

"Don't mention that name!" He stood up abruptly. "Don't be like Mother. I have changed three in the space of three weeks and I don't intend to employ another. You know," he continued, "it's not strange that you should ask me that question. I was asked that same question recently and I wasn't vexed but rather anxious and failed to address the matter properly. I did some research on the matter of Nannies and fathering and I discovered some very interesting things. Robert Blodgett a writer lecturer and author of Family First: Tales of a Working Father (Grande Press) said that few believe that a father would choose family, over career. He recently saw a powerful politician from Washington who, though he received no praise, walked away from a lucrative career to take care of his family. I'm just a simple banana farmer. Why shouldn't I? It's a matter of choice. Plus, I'm not giving up my business as a farmer, I'm taking leave."

"I'm not quarrelling with you, but I've never seen you in this light."

"Well, there are many things that have changed for the better since we last communicated. You know just talking to you reminds me of some of the things I read. You know I see why you would speak like that.

In one case, a Maryland state trooper successfully sued for being denied leave as a primary caregiver for his child," wrote Blodgett. The trooper was told by his supervisor that "God made women to have babies, and, unless he could have a baby, there is no way he could be the primary care (giver)." As a man, he was not expected to play that role. That is why he said that "Only 13 percent of companies offer paid paternity leave." "Do you see what I am saying Daphne? Well I am going to be a mother and father to Lily." His voice rose a few notches. When he composed himself, he asked her, "Now are you going to help me or not?"

"I am glad the old perception has changed, for old dogs can be taught new tricks."

"So, is that a yes?"

"Of course, I will help you. Do you think I am still stupid?" "Come on Daphne, you know I didn't mean that. It was only my way of getting back at Father."

"Well I knew you wanted my help in one way or the other so that is why I came in the first place, and secondly, it is a long time since we had some time together."

"Thank you, Daphne; You won't regret it."

Daphne was three years younger than Jerry. She had a darker cool complexion with black low-cut hair and bright eyes. She stood at five feet seven inches tall and weigh one hundred and thirty- six pounds. Daphne was a charming young woman who spent most of her time working. She was John's baby girl. She never left home and occupied the same bedroom from she was a child even when she went to nursing school. She rode the bus back and forth. Even at her age she was never wrong in John's sight.

Daphne didn't sleep well that night. She lay awake for much of the time. Her mind recaptured much of her teenage years. She had said yes to Jerry, but she felt a tinge of uneasiness even though she worked with children every day. She stared up at the ceiling and remembered how Jerry made fun at her expense. He called her Daphy Duck, Daphy Doodle and Dumb Daphy. He criticized her feet and everything she did. For that and other reasons, he never had the support of his stepfather. Daphne was glad when she left home to go to nursing school. And though many years had passed, she suddenly felt a strange weight of apprehension. On the contrary, Lily didn't cry or wake up all night, but Jerry was always awake.

At 2 AM, his knock, on Daphne's room door jolted her.

"Is that you Jerry?" She got up and looked at the clock. It was 2.00am.

"Yes."

She opened the door.

"I couldn't sleep. I was heading for the refrigerator when I saw your light on, so I decided to see if you were alright."

"Well you know that I've always slept with my light on. I still haven't changed."

"May I come in?"

"As a matter of fact, I believe that I could do well with a cup of hot chocolate myself. How about you?" and she was walking through the door as she whipped on her robe.

"I suppose one would do me no harm," he said, as he stood aside for her to pass.

They headed for the kitchen. Jerry opened the door and turned on the light as Daphne paused. There was a sense of neatness about the room. There was meticulous care in the way everything was placed. He moved toward the store. She stilled him with a stiff hand. She lifted the white enamel kettle from the stove. It was filled with water. She replaced it, turned on the burner and soon it was humming until it whistled. It was easy to find everything. Tea and a box of crackers were close at hand. She prepared chocolate for herself flavoured with nutmeg and cinnamon and a cup of tea for Jerry. They sipped, crackled on their crackers, and chatted.

"So, what kept you awake?"

"Oh nothing, I was just thinking." "Thinking about?"

"Nothing much."

"Come on Jerry, we are adults now." Jerry laughed. "You wouldn't believe it."

Daphne laughed as well, she found it intriguing. She took over the questioning; She was really enjoying herself.

"I don't suppose that you not being able to sleep, had anything to do with our silly teenage rivalry?" Asked Daphne.

"So that was indeed your problem Daphne?" "Not at all."

"Well, well here we go."

"So why did you bring it up," "Bring it up?" "Did I? Admit it Daphne." "Admit what? That was your problem too."

"I'm sure that I understand you. You thought that I hadn't changed and probably at some time I would assert that little sister, bigger brother stuff," he said.

"Why should I Jerry? I'm surprised that you even dare to think that way."

"It certainly begs that simple question for the sake of this conversation. Does older and bigger mean more matured? And is the opposite true?"

"Oh no. But we all delve into our past on occasions like this for various reasons. For some people, it's out of fear and uncertainty; for others, it's a means to an end. It is all a part of the process of analyzing where we are coming from and where we are going." Daphne said.

"Certainly, the latter was merely my concern." "What was yours?"

"Well Daphne, you could say we were barking up the same tree." "You have not missed by much."

"I'm sure you didn't overlook the fact that, I remain your bigger brother and you are now my big sister." They finished their last sips of tea and stood. Jerry reached out and hugged her. "Thank you for coming big sister. I am very thankful."

He was about to open the kitchen door when Daphne stopped him. "Aren't we forgetting one important thing?"

"What's that?"

"What I'm here for? What are the plans? How do we proceed?" "Could we do this in the morning Daphne, say over breakfast?" "Ok."

It was 5:30 AM when Jerry awoke. Daphne followed at 6 AM. Jerry had breakfast ready. He prepared boiled green bananas, steamed cabbage, liver, and fresh orange juice. He had tea and Daphne had hot spicy chocolate as usual. Lily slept soundly so they had time to plan. Daphne would demonstrate everything and then Jerry would repeat each. Jerry would explain what he already knew, and Daphne would agree or disagree and make corrections where necessary. Most of what she did was made extremely easy because Jerry knew some but just lacked the confidence to do them. However, because of his willingness to learn, they all seemed easy. She demonstrated how he should bathe Lily, change her clothes, clean her ears and tongue, and cut her nails. Even those things Jerry understood before, but he enjoyed watching Daphne doing them. She reminded him to stick a little calendar on the refrigerator door and mark special dates such as days of her appointments with her paediatrician. He should continue to use the timer to remind him when to feed her and remember to boil water for her. He should sterilize her rag in the microwave for twenty-five seconds, three times per week.

Above all else, she cautioned him against lifting her up every time she cried.

"Check to see if she wets herself and then change her, instead of scooping her up in your arms. You will create a habit that you'll certainly regret." Then she paused and looked at him. "Jerry, you are not only a big brother but a good student."

"Thank you, big Sister. This is quite a compliment coming from you."

Two weeks later Daphne packed and was ready to move on. It was a Friday afternoon. Jerry had just returned from the supermarket with groceries.

"Jerry, it is time to go," she said in a beautiful feminine tone. "I will be leaving tomorrow."

"Already?"

"I must return home to get through some stuff before I go back to work on Monday. I've been here for two weeks."

"How time flies. I was just getting used to having you around. This was the same thing I said to mother before she left."The difference is, I didn't gain as much as I do now.

That night before Jerry went to bed he packed a carton box of foodstuff and fresh fruits and vegetables for her. He woke early next morning and placed it into the van for her. Daphne was busy bathing and tidying Lily. She had become so attached to her that she found herself wiping tears.

"You are going to be a fine young lady. One day I will come back to see you; you will be beautiful, talented, and independent."

Jerry came and stood by the door. She hugged him tightly, he picked up her bags and walked out of the room.

"Jerry," she reached out to him in a, departing mood, sniffling, laughing and wiping her nose.

"I can see that you are ready."

"Yes, I'm; it is time to go." She ran back and hugged him again. "I love you, big brother." She smiled nervously.

"I love you too big sister. Here, this is for you."

She took the envelope he held out to her and opened it. "Jerry, I didn't charge you." She took out $500.00 from his overly generous gift and gave the envelope back to him.

"You keep this. Please buy something special for Lily." She extended her hand to him. He drew her into a close embrace.

"Goodbye big sister."

She closed her eyes and took a deep breath. "Good bye big brother."

He opened the door of the van and she entered. Dave pulled away over the hill and Jerry watched until they were out of sight.

Chapter 4

Jerry went back inside to continue his big dream of fathering and mothering Lily. He loved her more dearly every day. He was more tender and compassionate, and Lily loved nothing more than to cuddle up in his arms and go to sleep. She grew prettier and alert and Jerry was very proud of her. Her first speech sound was a whole sentence: "My daddy." This took Jerry by surprise. He had much more coming. And did they have a wonderful time together. Nothing was more precious than for her daddy to carry her on his back up and down the hallway.

By age three she was probably far more advanced than all the children around. She could dress herself properly and tie her shoe laces, better than most children her age. She had an excellent memory. She could listen attentively for thirty even thirty-five minutes when Daddy read to her. She was able to ask and answer intelligent questions. She had very excellent hand and eye coordination so, she could colour pictures within margins and she was very good at special relationship. Jerry taught her many of these through songs and rhymes.

He taught her:" "In to the pond out of the pond, to show relationship between inside and outside. "Here we go around, the mulberry bush," demonstrated circular movement, and "Upstairs, downstairs" to teach up and down. They would walk around and step over objects, bend under the table which she enjoyed immensely.

Daddy would say: "Woops, mind your head." And before she did she would say: "Woops Daddy, mind your head." All this knowledge Jerry transferred to paper so, she knew simple antonyms and synonyms, thus contributing to a well-developed vocabulary. He insisted on home schooling her until her fourth birthday.

It is always possible for most parents to answer baby's questions effectively. The questions of a three- and five-year-old child should be no different. It is rare that the odd question should puzzle adults. However, this was not the case when Lily asked: "Daddy, why did God take away Mommy so early?"

Of course, the first seven words would have been quite in order but 'so early.' This certainly startled him. Jerry took a few seconds to compose himself and turned over the question in his mind. He pulled out one of her story books from the set and was about to evade the direct answer, when she decided to make it easy, so it seemed, to give him more time.

"Maybe I was very little." Whatever that really meant, it gave Jerry time to relax and decided how best to answer. He explained the accident and death as carefully as he could without being too graphic. Lily fell asleep at the point when he explained that they were hospitalized. Jerry covered her with a blanket, kissed her on her forehead and turned off the light. He went to bed that night counting his blessings for this very special child.

The year went by rapidly. Summer stretched on long and interesting. Lily was registered at St. Peter's Preparatory Christian school one year in advance to ensure that she got a place. Daddy had gotten her package in the mail and was ready to make preparation for school. One Friday evening, Daddy told her of plans for the next day to go to Montego Bay to shop. Although she had never gone shopping in the city with him she was excited. That night he tucked her in bed early and carefully laid out the clothes she would wear. The next morning, however, he was surprised to hear her early splashing in the bathroom. She didn't wait but started to bathe, so Daddy went and helped her.

The journey to the city was pleasant enough until they came to the spot where he and Zell had met in the accident, but he bravely proceeded as he fought back his emotion. In Montego Bay, Lily noticed everything and asked many questions. She asked about buildings and signs, and she was fascinated by the number of different cars that passed up and down the main street. Then it was time to pick out uniforms. Daddy showed her the colour and she just pick up a bunch of uniforms and brought them to her dad. "No, no baby you have to pick out your size." Size," she repeated. "Yes, the one that fits you" So Jerry picked up three pairs, one extra-large, one that is too small and one that fits just right. When he tried to put on the very small one she said this one is tight. Then he tried on the extra-large and she found it funny, she could not move about with it. "You see this is too large." Then he tried the one that fitted her properly. She said: "O o," And walked away.

When they returned home, she requested to try on the uniforms.

She said: "Daddy this uniform does not fit." So, he explained: that they were perfectly fitting for he didn't want her to grow out of those clothes in a few months. Then Daddy would have to buy another set and throw away the ones you grow out of. She nodded her head as if she understood.

It was an exciting moment on that September morning, when Lily started attending St. Peters Prep school. It was her birthday. The atmosphere was perfect. The sun was shining brightly over Tumba's Valley, but it was tempered by a cool breeze that came from the river. He waited on Dave to transport them, but he delayed.

Jerry continued to lease the farm until Lily started school. Even then he never took up farming full time, Dave was his right-hand man who was in charge of everything. He was efficient, and Jerry trusted him. The plantation flourished under his care. Twice Jerry was farmer of the year, but he gave all the credit to Dave. Dave expanded the plantation, hired new workers and handled the responsibility very well. He was very busy'

"Where is Dave? He should be back already." Lily hopped on one leg and called Jerry to look at her, but he seemed a bit distracted. "Dave should be back already. Come Lily, we'll walk to school."

This was to Lily's delight. She hopped and skipped all the way. She stumbled once and fell, however she got up immediately. She was just about to cry. She stuck out her hand to show her muddy little fingers, but Jerry 's compassionate voice, changed her mood.

"Oh, dear me; you fell! Oh, my darling you dirty your hand." He kissed her on the back of her muddy hand. "Let Daddy help you."

"Look Daddy, I dirty my clothes. My new uniform is dirty." "Don't worry." Jerry wiped her hands and kissed them. She looked at him affectionately. A radiant smile broke on her lips. Jerry proceeded to clean the spot of mud from her dress. "There," he said. "See, it is not so bad."

She gave him a curious look of admiration and they both started to laugh. "O dear, me you fell!" She made fun of her daddy and they both found it funny.

Lily's first day at school brought fun and excitement to everyone. The children and their teachers adored her. She was a little spark that kindled a real spirit of enjoyment. Her class was a buzz of excitement the likes of which the school had never seen before. New students were given opportunity to perform on their birthday.

It so happened, that it Lily's Birthday. Her singing and very good reading motivated the transmission of a quick note to the principal's office. The principal came in time to hear her telling her favourite story: "The Baby in the Basket." This story depicted an excerpt from the life of the Hebrews in captivity in Egypt some 4000 years ago. The king, Pharaoh, perceived that the Hebrews, now Israel, were multiplying too fast and would probably overthrow his nation so, he ordered that all males should be killed at birth. One adventurous mother defied the odds and hid her wonderful child in a basket in the River Jordan.

By an act of divine intervention as described by many bible scholars and commentators, he became Pharaoh's son, and his original mother became his nurse. He later became the instrument used by the Almighty to deliver the Israelites from bondage, had several personal encounters with his divine master, wrote the Pentateuch, the first five books of the Holy Bible, including the ten commandments and the laws.

According to some scholars Moses was arguably one of the greatest leaders of all time. Additionally, he was probably the first man to establish what many leadership proponent, call the Metro Principles, which is a forerunner of the fundamental leadership structure. Leaders of modern leadership structure site this story as they develop their own theory. As they referred, to (Numbers 18:19-26).

As Lily continued her episode, she answered a child's question on whether little Baby Moses was afraid. "No," she replied. "His mother was watching him." The principal and the class clapped and sang Happy Birthday to her. It was her special day.

It wasn't purely a coincidence that she answered with such ease, but she had learned it from example. One day Jerry took her to the stream behind their house to play in the water. Delightfully Lily floated paper boats down the stream and ran alongside the stream to watch them sail gracefully as she and Dad sang:

> *"I have a little paper boat.*
> *A tiny little paper boat*
> *I float it down, away down-stream*
> *So far Away*
> *So far away; so far away, it sales from me."*

Sometimes Daddy would run with her and cheer for the winning boat. Then with joyful heart he sometimes lifted her on his shoulder and ran with her. It was on one of these occasions when one of her favourite boats got stuck in the weeds. The riverbed widens, and the water moves slowly. That was where he drew his perfect example to explain why Baby Moses didn't float downstream.

That evening Jerry picked her up from school himself. It was a joy to see her run freely and unhindered. She jumped on stage to entertain a group of children. Jerry stood some distance away and watched so as not to distract her. He was surprised when he saw the ease with which she related to all of them as they changed from one ring game to another. They sang "Hot cross bun. Hot cross bun, one for penny, two for penny, Hot cross bun." Some of these nursery rhymes were those he taught her at home. When he beckoned for her to leave, she called out: "One more Daddy, one more." And patiently Daddy waited for her, then all the children accompanied her to Jerry's pickup truck and ran inside the compound along the road as she drove away.

Their journey home was as pleasant as the sunny September afternoon. The bumpy rugged stone road was dotted with pot holes; some filled with muddy water rocked the little truck. The subsequent rocking of the slow- moving vehicle, didn't diminish Lily's enthusiasm and excitement about her day. As, Daddy deliberately perked himself up to be entertained by his little heaven on earth. She told him everything and he absorbed it like a sponge.

Dinner was already prepared before Daddy went to pick her up. Lily had her bath and was ready for dinner. She skipped two classes Kindergarten and grade one. At that time, she was reading very well. Three years later, a competition was held in memory of her mother who had died tragically. Daddy was accused of nepotism."How could I be accused of nepotism. All I did was to take Lily to the school for practice and of course I helped her at home as all normal parent would.

To break the news to Lily that she couldn't participate further was a big strain on Daddy. Yet, he was made to count his fortune.

When he attempted to explain to Lily, she just said, "I know Daddy, don't worry about it. I will participate next year." because she was told at school. As it turned out, Lily didn't participate the next year either and like an evil spell, as some of her classmates describe, she was hospitalized with a bout of Pneumonia. Therefore, as she was physically unable, and for a peaceful life, Daddy didn't pursue the matter. Pneumococcal pneumonia is not a cold or the flu. It's an illness that is caused by Streptococcus pneumoniae, a common bacteria, that can be spread from person to person through a cough or touch. These bacteria can cause part of the lung to become inflamed and fill up with mucus, making it harder to breathe. It started one afternoon when she came from school. She came down with a cough and high fever. Daddy called her paediatrician who asked him to bring her to the hospital where he met them. She was immediately given breathing treatment and an injection counteract the symptoms. After resting for five days in the hospital she was released, and Daddy took her home.

She recovered from her illness and had soon regained her usual disposition. Her elementary years were outstandingly good. Therefore, Daddy had high hopes that her prospect in high school was very good. Yet, for some strange and unbelievable reason she failed the Common Entrance Examination that would have given her access or transfer her to the High school. Fortunately, her birth day would be on September 3rd the next school year, therefore she could spend another year in grade six in the Elementary school. "This was the strangest occurrence I have ever seen," her principal remarked about her failure. However, she surely didn't make the same mistake next year. She got a full scholarship, all expenses paid.

The next three years of Lily's school was very difficult. It was hard to imagine that a student of such promise, who never got detentions in Elementary school, who constantly made the Principal's Honour Roll, could wind up becoming such a problem student in the junior years of High school.

It started late summer. She was thirteen years old. For many days, she was barricaded in her room, totally preoccupied. She remained in her room for extended hours. She ate sparingly and listened constantly to Rock Music. This Daddy couldn't understand. She emerged only if she needed water or a drink from the refrigerator; and she avoided coming out when Daddy was in the living room. What was strange was that she lost her impetus for reading and it seemed that she replaced it with music, loud music.

She was growing up. This Daddy knew. For, she no longer sat with him in the evenings when he came home, nor did she leave her door open any longer. She always locked it. Yet Daddy tried to be comfortable with locking her door. Of course, she was a young lady now. Daddy thought she needed her privacy, but when she locked her door before going into the bathroom, he became quite alarmed. That meant he shouldn't go in her room period. He sensed that, and he didn't want to upset her any further.

On the other hand, he had never raised a daughter before, so he hardly knew what to expect. He was taken by surprise, he never saw this coming. This was not anything like when she was a baby. Then, he had the luxury of calling her baby names. He would take her on his back and trot around in the house. He remembered her little voice saying, "Go horsey." Now that she was growing up, he was at a loss as to how to deal with some of her ways. When her music became too loud he would bang on the wall for her to turn it down.

It was this same attitude that spilled over into high school. At first, she started out brilliantly. Yet, somehow along the way in the first year, she made a drastic shift. It started during the period of Lent. The congregation of Merton Town Methodist church was observing certain religious rights. This was the period when some Christians abstained from eating certain foods and doing certain activities nearing the crucifixion of Christ. Listening to rock music was considered a violation of that sacred time. Daddy demanded that she observe this tradition by choosing to listen to a different kind of music and their first conflict began. Therefore, she entered the last semester in a bad mood. She rebelled against his penalizing her by stopping her from listening to her Rock music. Therefore, school was the farthest thing from her mind, when the new school term began at the end of the Easter holiday.

What Daddy and her teachers didn't question was, the reason for this compulsive behaviour. How could she suddenly become so unproductive and unwilling? And no one seemed to care enough to investigate. How could his smart Lily change so drastically in only a few short months? Daddy could trace the date back to the anniversary of her Mother's death. She was merely thirteen, going fourteen years old. They had observed a candlelight ceremony in honour of Zelda's death, but she never went. Since Dave Carter, his hired foreman, now in his late forties, and his wife Barbara thirty-eight, shared a back room on the house, he thought it was ok to go to a midnight cry: a prayer meeting at his church; which started at 9.00 pm. and ended at 12.00 midnight. That again she refused to go. The next day he and Dave went to the city to a meeting at the All Island Banana Growers Boxing Plant, where all the growers met to ward off a pending strike by unionized laborers who worked in the Banana Industry, for better remuneration.

Clearly, he could remember if he bothered to, that when he returned, she never acted like her normal self. Her face was tear-stained, it seemed that she was crying. Dave or his wife hadn't visited her. Thus, they had no clue of what caused of her behaviour. This was when she began locking herself in her room. This was the recipe for disaster and it was quickly tested when she got to school. That disaster did strike. It was April 16th, was the start of the third nine week of school. The semester had barely started. Dave dropped her off at school. At 11.00 a.m. Daddy received a telephone call from the school. He was summoned to a meeting in the principal's office. Surely this must be some routine matter. Why would he have to discuss trivial matters in the middle of the day?

Now he was upset. On the first day of school, parents should not be called away from their jobs in the middle of the day, unless it was a matter of extreme urgency. It was a busy day for him.

A freak storm had leveled several acres of his banana crop and he had laborers harvesting and chopping up and dumping and burning unwanted litter in the field. This was to prevent contamination of the banana field from disease and infestation that could affect the next crop. He was sure that he would just clarify the simple matter whatever it was and got back to his business.

So quickly, he was at school, his brown eyes reflecting his disgust. He wore his usual banana stained outfit but well laundered. His tall sleeve shirt rolled up to his elbow revealing gray hair over his copper brown brawny hands. His heavy brown leather boots had streaks of mud around the edge of the sole. He was clean shaved, and his fifty- five years old gray hair showed up around the edge of his green army coloured cap. It was the first day school. There was nothing to cause alarm. Yet to his surprise, a defiant Lily was sitting on a chair near the principal's office sobbing. A police officer engaged the principal in a conversation. Daddy made giant steps to cross the room. He couldn't interpret the look on Lily's face, but she seemed both frightened and upset. Lily, one hundred and fifteen-pound thirteen-year-old, and quite tall for her age, merely looked up at him to show her tear stained dark brown face. She was dressed in a baby blue silk and satin blouse and refine khaki-like short pants revealing her long legs. Her hair was braided and she wore a blue head band to keep her braids in place. She wore blue sneakers to complement her uniform. She was well dressed but in trouble.

There was another stick-thin Hispanic girl, fair in complexion about her age, and a wiry shaped woman with a big bust who seemed to be her mother, sitting on another chair on the opposite side from her. The girl was similarly dressed like Lily but her long dark hair spread over her shoulders. She had bluish green eyes and shiny white teeth. The wiry woman Hispanic, was dressed in black with a pearl necklace through which she kept running her fingers to move the beads around. Her face revealed the painstaking effort of makeup. She hid her eyes behind sunglasses. They all had one thing in common: a puzzled questioning look, on their faces. But Lily's pale countenance, begged for sympathy. At that moment Daddy decided that something must be wrong. There was something wrong indeed. The other girl seemed quite relax and smiling as if she had no cause to worry. But Lily carried the weight of the world on her slumped shoulders.

The ten minutes wait appeared endless. The principal appeared, middle aged, and dressed in a tailored sober gray tall sleeve round neck suit, with three one cent size black buttons running down the center from her neck to her solar plexus. Her hair was combed backward and pinned in a bun at the back of her head. She carried an authoritative posture. She picked up the telephone and called her secretary. "Please send them in," She sounded impatient. She spoke in polite English, a refined and polished voice. Both parents eyed each other. The youngsters walked hesitantly but they completed the journey, though not in record time, but before Mrs. Blagrove sounded an alarm for security to bring them in. They shuffled in and sat beside each parent. The police officer stood but not with the intention of intimidating them. He was stately, with broad shoulders, dressed in black pants with a two and a half inch, red stripe along the sides of his pants over patent leather boots. He wore a short sleeve stripe white shirt firmly tucked in his pants with a black sheened leather belt supporting a red comer band.

"I can tell how it happened, Mrs. Blagrove," Lily volunteered, not wanting her classmate Shana to speak, less she should say something she didn't want her Daddy to hear.

"You just wait a moment young lady," Mrs. Blagrove interrupted. "But I can tell you," she protested. "I didn't mean to." And tears brimmed and streaked down her face.

"Ok young lady, you know you are in big trouble already, so you don't make things worse. And you too, Miss!" She snapped at the other girl who was smiling. "Coming in my office and sitting dry eyed." Mrs. Blagrove flung one stare in her direction, and then looked in one sweep at the police officer, Lily, and both parents. Before she looked at Shana again. By then she joined Lily in her pity party, and both girls were sobbing. Mrs. Blagrove picked up a referral from her desk and read the contents aloud as recorded by the class teacher. Both girls had a quarrel in class that became disruptive. Lily grabbed the girl by her hair and threatened to wring her neck. The girl in turn slapped her and they began to fight, so the teacher had to restrain both girls. Obviously, Lily vehemently objected because she didn't get to return the blow, so she began to cry hysterically and wouldn't conform to any discipline, so the school police was called.

Hearing this, Daddy was appalled. "You were fighting?"

Lily buried her head in her lap. Shana covered her face with her palms and shared the similar grief. They had disappointed their parents. Shana's mother spoke in Spanish, to which Mrs. Blagrove answered "Sí," in response. The police stood nearby. These girls didn't need any spanking. But Lily watched Mrs. Blagrove and saw her take up the strap several times, but she sensed that the presence of their parents wouldn't approve spanking. One look from both their parents and they had shed enough tears to convince everyone that they were sorry.

It was during mathematics class. The story went wild. For whatever the unexplained reason, Shana went into Lily's bag without permission. Lily grabbed her hair and yanked her head and called her nosy. Shana, without thinking of the consequences, slapped Lily and that threw oil on the fire. The fight ensued. Both girls were reprimanded and sent home with their parents for two days suspension.

Chapter 5

The journey home was probably the longest Daddy had ever driven on that route. He drove in silence. Only his jaws kept moving. Lily had no more tears to shed, but she occasionally snuffled to keep Daddy reminded of her sincerity. Daddy found that there were more important things to do than returning to the tasks that his hired hands could do. The truck slowly rocked and bumped over the driveway and came to a stop in front of the house. Lily tried to open the door to get out, but Daddy stretched out his hand and stopped her. She buried her face in her palms again and began to cry.

Jerry had always blamed himself for Zell's death. He slumped his shoulders, twitched uncomfortably but said nothing. He screamed inwardly, that if he had made taking her to the hospital a priority, he would have put off the other things he was doing down at the farm. As a result, he would've driven her to the hospital before peak hours. He remembered the words Zell had spoken: "You know what the doctor said. "Why do you take chances? You know what the traffic situation is like during this time of the day." He bowed his head as if a weight was set on his neck. Her words burned deep in his conscious mind. Lily continued her snuffling. When she saw her Daddy's posture she sobbed even louder.

The mid- afternoon sun bore down on the truck parked in front of the house. Dave's wife, holding her grandchild in her hand, came to the side of the house and looked. The farm hands came passing by for their lunch break. Everyone looked on with concern. Even the fruit trees: the June-plum, the banana, and mango seemed to still their motion in the quiet atmosphere, as if to give a listen ear. Not even the slightest breeze ruffled their leaves. Since all nature was seemingly curious, and competing for Daddy's attention, he seemed to satisfy their curiosity as he opened the door and said to Lily: "I will talk to you later," and suddenly a gust of wind stirred and woke them up. It blew a farm hand's hat off her head, and it was comical to watch her hat escaped from her in the wind as she tried to catch it. Lily hurried to her room and closed the door.

Daddy didn't return to work for the rest of the day. He gave the workers the rest of the day off as well. He sat on the veranda in his usual chair and he looked out and up the road, and across the patch of catch crop growing on the right side of the road leading up the driveway. He usually sat in this spot when he was contemplative. The long fifteen-foot veranda glistened with red stained polish, stretched from north to south. The north side was very low and led into a room entered through a double door on the right. Four posts painted red with white stripes on each of the four corners supported the weight of the roof. Around the veranda a decorated wall that was erected when Lily started walking completed the finished work. In front of the one flight step to enter the veranda, the lone dog curled on a mat. And two of Daddy's steps across the veranda led into the living room. The southern end was about four to five feet high. This end overlooked the place where Zelda's body was laid to rest. When Daddy turned his chair toward the south contemplatively, it always appeared as if he was having a conversation with her.

The evening shadows lengthened, birds flew across the sky out of sight. The hens gathered their chicks to their roost, and bugs, beetles, and frogs began their long discordant sounding lyrics that signalled nightfall. A heavy slumber came over Daddy and he succumbed to the will of nature in the dim twilight. In his deep slumber, he relived the hours he spent in the hospital after the accident.

It was only 7 p.m. "Oh my head, Zell! Is Zell alright? Where am I?" "Please Mr. Parks," he heard, "take it easy. You had a very bad accident. Don't get upset again." It appeared as if he sank in the bed and was going through so he held onto the rails as he listened to the nurse.

"Accident?" He tossed restlessly in his chair as he talked to himself. Lily heard and came to look at what was happening to her Daddy, saw him struggling in his sleep, and woke him up. "Daddy," she called to him.

"Oh, my child, I was having this awful dream." She pulled up a chair and sat beside him. "Dream? What were you dreaming about?" She asked." O my child it was horrible. It was the accident that took your mother's life when you were born. Do you think that you can listen to the full story? I believed you are matured enough to understand. Are you sure you will not get upset and blame Daddy?" "I will try." By then she knew he was fully awake. He hugged her and poured out the story. I meant to have told you sometime, but I was not sure that you were ready to handle it. Lily listened attentively as Daddy held her close. He felt the tension in here body released with sudden tears as she sobbed.

You see my child Mom died to preserve your life. It was like what scientists called a Metamorphosis, the change of a person into a completely different one, by natural or supernatural means. She died, but in the process, changed to be you. The Devil meant to kill both of you, but God resisted his attack, to steal, both of you from me. The doctor said if he had tried to save both you and your mother's life, you both would have died. (Genesis 50:20): So, what the Devil meant for evil God turned it around for good. Here you are, the result of this, this. "tragedy" she said. Yes, my dear it was a tragedy but here you are a beautiful, image of your mother, you are bright, articulate and very smart. Do you believe that you can forgive your Daddy? O Daddy she sunk her head in his right side, then looked up in his face. "Everybody will blame you for staying down at the farm too long. But I know you would never do anything to hurt Mummy. Probably if you had come earlier the accident would've happened just the same." O., my child I am glad that you see it that way. God could have prevented it, but he allowed it to happen. Nothing happens to his children unless He allows it. (Psalm 17:8) says: He Keeps us as the apple of His eye and He hides me in the shadow of His wings. His children live as redeemed people. However, he put off the conversation of her behaviour at school because he believed that she had enough for one day. So, they retired to bed and promised to resume r conversation about her behaviour the following day.

Neither father nor child had a good sleep that night. Lily went to bed regretting that she never had a mother although she loved her Daddy dearly. Yet she could not share everything with him. On the one hand, she believed that if her mother was alive she could talk to her about her life story. She would know how she overcame her ordeal of the rape and how did she manage to forgive her parents. Likewise, she would certainly see her side of the story when Shana assaulted her at school that day. Daddy on the other hand, could not stop blaming himself for Zell's death. He sobbed and mourned himself to sleep. However, when daylight broke the next morning brought new refreshing light. Jerry looked through his window to the east and saw the sun rising, It was splendid to see the morning coming up over those green hills and glowing through those sharp top of the June-plum tree. He remembered the vow he made in the hospital. He remembered when Daphne left how elated he felt to continue his role as single parent, he fetched himself a cup of coffee, looked at himself in the mirror and said Today is a new beginning, I need a fresh start. He put down his cup on the dresser before the mirror, opened the window, looked towards Zelda's tomb and said: "Girl I wash my soul in the beauty of this sunshine. I miss you, but I will carry on."

He prepared breakfast until Lily awoke. They ate and began their conversation. Jerry didn't rant or rave at her, but his fatherly instinct took over and he listened to her side of the story and gave her his firm opinion. He told her the girl had no right to go in her bag, but that didn't give Lily the authority to defend herself with violence. He showed her that she had the power to change the situation, but she blew it when she yanked Shana's head. He told her: "A soft or gentle answer turns away wrath; but harsh words or action stirs up anger." (Proverbs15:1) She didn't reply, fearing that she would've gotten into more trouble. Lily was totally subdued and went to bed feeling very uncomfortable in her spirit. While she accepted Daddy's argument, she maintained that if she had the chance to slap Shana it would've made her felt better. Thus, she decided that in the future she would draw first blood.

Yet, Jerry, planned to reward her for her efforts in the competition which she won two years after her illness. He was very proud of her as he watched her performance. Each competitor was asked to read three books during the summer. For the competition, each participant competed at three levels; in spelling, written, and oral comprehension. She got help from her dad as well as the principal of the school. When all other teachers were on vacation; Jerry would drop her off at school in the mornings and pick her up at 12.00 pm. As a result, she successfully aced the test. Her victory made not only her daddy and the principal proud, but all the readers of the Jamaican Sunday Gleaner News Paper Publication that weekend as she was the featured guest. However, Jerry delayed her present until her sixteenth birthday. One spring, reaching into summer, Jerry occupied his time very productively on his return home each day. He worked on his master plan to reward her not just for her performance in the competition, but as a symbolic gesture that spotlight the cause of why the name Lily was given to her and the very existence of her being Lily. Therefore, he worked diligently preparing flower beds and planting flowers and vegetables of all kinds. Soon the garden was a picture of exotic vegetables and flowering hybrid rose bushes, tulips, marigolds, and zinnia. The gladiolus, lily which embodies strength of character, sincerity, and moral integrity was his favourite. This he planted in the center of the garden which represents the heart and the center of our life. Just like our physical hearts are vital to our physical life, so our spiritual heart to our relationship with the Eternal. Just as we all have physical hearts, we all have spiritual and emotional heart. Jesus (and others in the Bible) often spoke of our heart in ways that just can't be describing our physical heart. "The heart is observed as a symbol for our emotions, for love, for deep-seated passions, for the center of our beings. It's where courage arises and the pain of hurt lingers." It is this heart by which we are saved. With the heart man believes unto righteousness.

Gladiolus are available in a wide range of colors, including white, pink, red, purple, yellow, orange, salmon, and green but the white gladiolus lily, was the most charming. He hoped to use that as an object lesson to teach Lily the sincerity and beauty of moral purity. Like the plant is spotlessly pure, so Jerry hoped his daughter would adopt her life to live a spotlessly, untarnished and morally sound. Therefore, he worked sometimes until way up until eight o'clock in the still bright afternoons of the long hot summer. He worked very hard during July and August, to meet the deadline for celebrating her 16th birthday on September 1st. He arranged the beds with adequate space to walk around them.

All during August, Jerry and Lily worked feverishly in the afternoons, mulching, watering the plants and weeding around them. At last, by the end of August, the flowers just seemed to burst in an array of colors. Vegetables were fit and ready in the most juicy and succulent clusters. Butterflies and wasps and other insects began to take interest and took notice of them.

Vegetables were ripe and ready to be picked.

Lily, red ox-heart tomatoes, string beans and cabbages folded hard.

On August 31st first, Lily arose very early and looked through her bedroom window and saw that the lily was in bloom. It had six beautiful white petals. Suddenly it dawned on her that the flower had her name. She went outside to admire the beauty it had to offer. She bent, smelled it, and touched it it's delicate petals gently with her fingers. "I am Lily; I have the name of a beautiful flower," she said. "Of course, I knew that, but now it just seems new as I think about it." Back inside, she logged into her PC and searched for lily and found some useful information about them. They are: "bulbous plant with large trumpet-shaped, typically fragrant, flowers on a tall, slender stem. Lilies have long been cultivated, some kinds being of symbolic importance and some used in perfume. Then she searched for the meaning of lily and observed the meaning to be: Dating as far back as 1580 B.C., when images of lilies were discovered in a villa in Crete and these majestic flowers have long held a role in ancient mythology. "Derived from the Greek word "Leiron," (generally assumed to refer to the white Madonna lily) The lily was revered by the Greeks that they believed it sprouted from the milk of Hera, the queen of the gods. Lilies are known to be the May birth flower, and the 30th wedding anniversary flower. While white lilies symbolize chastity and virtue – and were the symbol of the Virgin Mary's purity and her role of Queen of the Angels. As other varieties became popular, they brought with them additional meanings and symbolism as well. Peruvian lilies, or Alstroemeria, represent friendship and devotion; white stargazer lilies express sympathy; and pink Alstroemeria stargazer lilies represent wealth and prosperity. Symbolizing humility and devotion, lilies are the 30th anniversary flower - while lily of the valley flowers are the 2nd wedding anniversary flower."

Strangely, at 14 she never desired to have a birthday party. She just never saw the need of putting her dad through the trouble. After reading the things her mother went through and her recent trouble at school, she just never wanted to be bothered, but the sixteenth birthday meant everything to her. Therefore, when she got out of bed, Dad had already fixed breakfast early, but he told her that he had a surprise for her. They had breakfast, and she wasn't expecting that her Dad would buy her a present after her bad behaviour at school. However, she volunteered to clear the table and wash the dishes. But Daddy said, "Allow them to remain until we get back, because there is something I want you to see."

Dad looked at her, as he stood anxious to go outside and not wanting to leave her behind. Finally, she left the kitchen and they both went outside to the flower garden. She wondered why they would go out to the garden so early. He never reaped vegetables or cut flowers so early. But he took her right to the center of garden and said "I planted this garden with you in mind. Your mother loved flowers and this Lily was her favourite. I want you to have it. Protect it and care it as she would care for you. Do you see how white and beautiful are its petals? So, let your behaviour be pure. Let it be free from malice or grudge, and let your conduct be untarnished and immaculate as this Lily." Lily was speechless. Imagine she had just researched and found out so many beautiful things about the lily, now her dad gave her, her own personal flower. She just hugged him and said "Thank you, dad. I will take good care of Her." He gave her big squeeze as well and they walked back inside.

Life had found that Grade 8 was not all sugar and spice. Writing was a real challenge. Writing argumentative essays was no cake walk. You had to write to certain specifications, which included reading multiple articles (at least three), grasping the two sides of the arguments, choosing one side and responding to it. This involved decoding the prompt, note taking, and evaluating the arguments to make your choice. Further, you must lay out a plan, present a thesis statement, cite at least three reasons for your choice (from at least two sources), cite evidence and present reasons to show how the evidence supports your claim before you start writing. Then you must also present a counter claim. In the test and exam, you have one and a half hours to accomplish the entire process, read it over, and present it. This was far from being easy. For this reason, writing was a real challenge to her. She worked extremely hard and she overcame her fears and pass with a B grade. She was elated that she still made the Principal's honour roll at the end of the semester.

It was Ninth grade that she bloomed. This was her final year and it brought new challenges. She was voted president of the Student Body. She took on two college level courses, plus her regular courses of Mathematics, Language Arts /Writing, Science, World Geography and French. She proved to be a truly good president, by following six basic principles: Firstly, she followed through on promises she had made during her campaign. All that she promised, she attempted to make them a reality. Some turned out well, but others not so well.

However, she did them openly, and when things didn't work well, all the naysayers were quick to pounce upon her. However, she had enough support to ward off their threats. Secondly, she tried to be present at most functions and participated in many. She was not a bystander. Thirdly she represented students' causes to the principal and her theme with vigor and full of interest, hence she created a bond with the students and was loved by all. As a result, she made it very easy to communicate to them to sell her ideas, build moral and team spirit among everyone. And, she had an aggressive fund-raising campaign. She had dances, sales at matches and teams of students selling popsicles, fudge, and cotton candy.

She was also successful in her class work. She utilized students help in carrying out research projects and providing her with material to complete her assignments to meet deadlines. She was quick to reward her helpers. Daddy always had to up her allowance, to meet extra cost but in the end, it paid off. She got all As and Bs on her college prep courses. Consequently, she was voted valedictorian, and earned a scholarship to the College of Arts Science and Technology where she study law and minor in Business and Communications Technology. Her intention was to practice law and be the voice   for young people who fell through the cracks like her mother and use her business skills to grow and manage her dad's business. She had a serious obsession against those who abuse children. Then, she purposed in her heart at all cost, to fight for their cause. At nights before she went to sleep, she placed a writing pad beside her bed to write down things that she visualized and think that were applicable for abused children. When she awoke in the nights she kept turning thoughts over and over in her mind. She could hear the voice of her mother calling her to action. In her address, at her graduation she revealed her intention why she wanted to practice law and used her mother as an illustration to make her point about why she wished to speak for the voiceless.

Chapter 6

Lily was elated about her flower and continued to admire it. She found out that the leaves were produced in the autumn or early spring in warm climates depending on the onset of rain and eventually die down by late spring. The bulb would then be dormant until late summer. The plant is not frost-tolerant, nor does it do well in tropical environments, since they require a dry resting period between leaf growth and flower spike production. Yet for some strange reason, destiny you may call it, her lily grew very well. One or two leafless stems arise from the bulb in the dry ground in early summer in its habitat in August. "The plant has a symbiotic relationship with Carpenter bees. It is also visited by noctuid moths. The relative importance of these animals as pollinators has not yet been established; however, Carpenter bees are thought to be the main pollinators."

As a result, she knew that the flower had a short life span and she wanted to preserve it. To that end, she cut it with its long stem and placed it in a beautiful vase and tepid water with floral preservative. She learned that for maximum enjoyment, she should cut the flower early in the morning. She removed the anthers to lengthen the life span of the flowers and avoid petal stain. She stored her cool room away from direct sun.

One day she noticed that the charming lily began to fade, so she started to reflect on what to do with her flower and then it hit her, that she could prolong the life span of the flower by preserving it. So, she did some research. The result was phenomenal.

Therefore, she opened the telephone book to the center and laid it open flat. She placed a sheet of blotting paper over one page of the book, then disassembled the blossom by pulling apart the petals from the bud carefully and slowly so as not to damage them. She placed each petal onto the blotting paper on the telephone book page as she removed each one. She spaced out the petals so that they weren't touching each other, then she covered it with another blotting paper closed the telephone directory and allowed it to process for about three weeks. Retrieved from (www.gardenguides.com › Flowers. How to Preserve Flower Petals). To her surprise, the petals became crisp and papery. She could still smell the delicate aroma of the flower and how nice it would be if she could preserve the scent as well. However, she proceeded to place them into a beautiful frame which she captioned "The Faded Flower." This picture became part of her life story for success, which she associated with her mother. She used it to illustrate the story of the tragedy of being raped, yet survived   to reproduce her, but faded in the process, by dying but under-went metamorphosis in her birth. Therefore, she assumed the privilege of becoming an advocate for the voiceless; those who were coerced to keep their mouth shut after injustice was trusted upon them. This was the dream her mother wanted to achieve.

Lily's life at the college of Arts Science and Technology and the University of the West Indies was one of mixed fortunes. Both colleges were in partnership. At UWI, she did her law degree, while at the former, she minored in Business administration. She contended with mixed fortune because she was always one up on her academic studies, but two down on relationships. As a committed young lawyer, she was president of the Law review board in her fourth year and she was good at it. At 20 she met her first true love. This was a totally new field to her. She always avoided boys for what happened to her mother. But there was always the type like her father Jerry with whom she would be attracted. Yet she could not detect these qualities of her father in the young man Raoul. He was an Accademia, full of knowledge and big desire, but he lacked grit, which was unfair to judge him on this single quality, since grit takes time to develop. He just could not articulate what his vision was.

He was slimly built, but you could pick him out of a crowd because of his distinguished side burns and neatly trimmed mustache below his thick rimmed glasses. He had a ready smile and friendly disposition. He always wore a well-tailored suit and tie. His destiny in real life, meant that he was seeing a preview of his future potential, but he vaguely could explain it. Lily didn't give him time to develop his thoughts and put meaning to what he believed. Yet there was something about his quiet demeanor that she thought was admirable and thought about sometimes at nights. Only if he was like her dad, 'O' she gasped one night as she drew the blanket over her head and went to sleep.

In her opinion, she was the total package, in the true sense of hard to get. In fact, she set the bar so high, that male companions were often frustrated just to get a date with her. She was rigid with her standards. She was the perfect persona of self-sufficiency of a brilliant, self-assured and confident young woman. Nothing fazed her, nothing frightened her. No male brought anything to the relationship table that she couldn't counteract or handle with calm resolve. She had an A prototype leadership character profile. She was very aggressive, business- like and non-nonsense in her action. If she went to a meeting she was ready to take charge. Therefore, she quietly and without embarrassment sent Raoul on his way. Yet, he wasn't ready to quit. He dreamed of the day when he would be on the opposite side of hard to get and this he pursued with diligence. He went to the same collage, though at separate times, graduated a head of his class and did his masters and PHD.

Lily firmly believed in male leadership. She believed that in the secular world nothing was wrong in leading male, but in the home, a man must lead. He must have plans and he must demonstrate them by his works. He couldn't seek to court her when he didn't have a vision for his life and the family he hoped to lead. This vision he needed to articulate clearly without reservation. She had nothing to do with boyfriend and girlfriend stuff. She was called to be a wife, a Proverbs 31 woman, a helpmate and the man must present her with the dream he had for their life. If he couldn't articulate that dream clearly without ambiguity, then he was wasting her time. Henceforth, many young men never looked in her direction. She had many social friends but no intimate ones. She was that serious in commitment as a young woman.

She strove to be number one in everything, whether it was in her studies or in sports. She was excellent in chess, dominoes, volleyball, swimming and debate, chiefly at the highest technical level. She chose only sports in which she could be dominant. During her college career she won several trophies, tournaments and was awarded many medals. She was sports woman of the year twice in her four years of college life. She was the ultimate package, a total all round student. This time around, she did not seek to get involve with student government. She had more important things to occupy her time, talent and her treasure. Therefore; she, with the aid of five friends launched a campaign on child abuse. They designed a slogan that read: "Child abuse stops now. Yesterday is passed, today is too late. Tomorrow is a tragedy waiting to get worse." They called themselves: "The Voice of the Voiceless;" Lily purposed to become an advocate to work with the abuse. She was consumed, with passion for voiceless people. She lay awake for hours thinking about little boys and girls who were abused and had no help. When she woke up it was the first thing on her mind. It all brought back to mind what she read about her mother in her little black book. This strengthened her desire to be a good advocate for the voiceless. She and her friends met over popcorn and a domino table and discovered that they all had the same itch, a passion and a longing for helping others.

First, she initiated talks with her Political representative, who was fired up about her cause and often used it in his campaign speech before and during his election campaign. However, after his election to office, he basically began to drag his feet over these matters. He ignored their calls, never kept appointments, so there seemed to be no way to get a hold of him. Lily tried to seek a platform to make her case before the House of Representative but was slighted in the initial process, because there were more pressing matters to deal with. There was budget to be tabled and there was violence especially among the young people which took priority.

The Sports Minister eventually got involved by implementing sports competitions and investing in sports infrastructure. Out of this came the All Island, Elementary and prep school, junior under 16, and under 19 cricket competitions. There was also the equivalent in soccer, and track and field competitions. Then there was a merger between Sports and Tourism, where one helped to promote the other. So, when there was no response from the elected minister, the text savvy girls all started to bombar the news and social media with ads and daily tweets. These efforts engaged the support of other lobbying groups, and a powerful law firm, "Steve and Steve Attorney at Law." The two brothers, both University of the West Indies graduates, grew up in the seventies when the young Michael Manley rocked the western hemisphere with his ideology of Democratic Socialism. They were both young men that Democratic Socialism burned in their conscience. These were men who would go out on a limb to defend the poor. They wore their convection on their sleeve. They were both lawyers and men who studied and practice the roles and responsibilities of advocacy and understood their roles. They didn't ask many questions, they just volunteered their time and resources. Jonathan was the older by four years. He was tall, stout and dressed like the Rastafarian cult but didn't support their religion. He could always be identified by his, gold teeth, dread locks and colorful African bandana head rap.

When you got close to him, he always smelled of expensive cologne. He wore gold chains and bracelets and spoke with a booming voice. His younger brother Steve Junior the iii, also sported dread locks, hung down his back. He was darker than John and shorter and he wore military camouflage outfit and cap like Fidel Castro. He was always dressed in leather boots and belt to match in colour. He was soft spoken and jovial, and his smile always exposed his very white teeth. He also sported expensive cologne and jewels. His eyes were dark and penetrating. He was more-friendly than Jonathan, and always seem to play second fiddle but they made a good partnership.

Not only did they get involved but subsequently, the public got involved as well. Then, that July 25, was a sad day in the capital city. Groups of lawless citizens launched a massive campaign. They blocked roads, burned tires, smashed windows of businesses, and looted without reservation. In their defense, they said they were supporting the cause of abused children. This was farthest from the truth. They could not be helping a just cause through lawless efforts. This view was voiced by the chief crime police officer Stone Wall Jackson, who rounded up several of them, and took them to jail.

As a result, they sought the services of Steve and Steve Law Firm. The Firm had then, hired Lily as a first -year lawyer. This case was one of the most unpopular in the history of criminal law in the country. Many people were critical of Steve and Steve for taking on the case and getting Lily involved. The public tried the case and found the defendants guilty before the case was officially tried. They held public demonstration, waved placards and chanted the slogan created by Lily and her associates. Therefore, when it was alleged that they would be represented by the law firm Steve and Steve and that Law firm employed Lily, they were simply irate. Some turned against her and regarded her as a traitor. They said she was betraying the very people she was trying to help.

This case involved two women and three men. They were charged with burglary, robbery, larceny and shooting with intent.

Lily was therefore baptized in the Criminal Justice System of the courts immediately. Fresh from being president of the Law Journal and Law Review Board of her College, and though young, she was afforded the opportunity to do the research, gather evidence, make a case and make preparation for her senior partners, a task that she thoroughly enjoyed. Thus, with confidence and courage she assumed her responsibility.

Yet, outrage of the public against her, wasn't a lost cause. The story went viral and attracted the attention of several local media outlets and foreign journalist who weighed in on the story. The BCC, Washington Pride and The Los Angel Times carried the story, but all the press, featured child abuse at length. It so happened that the government was forced to launch a thorough investigation into the matter regarding childhood abuse, funding of foster homes, and the care given daily to children in institutional homes, plus how they could minimize the effects on those who were exposed to violence. Interestingly, it took six weeks to name a committee to do the job.

Then the report should be tabled in Parliament in nine months, yet one year passed. So, when a year and six months was approaching, a special radio program employing the effects of roving microphone on an early morning broadcast, during Monday at peak hours, caused some buzz. They asked the simple question: "Do you think the committee will get the job done on time?" Most answers were positive because for once, the public had made demands on the government and they stood by their word much to their annoyance. So much so, that, within three days following the buzz in the street, two of the leading newspapers reported contrasting articles. The one appeared on Wednesday, and was critical of the government, because the minister of Children's affairs threatened to make heads roll. This prompted the resignation of the manager Children Services, followed by several other workers.

Consequently, the move of resignations drew sharp reaction from the public. It meant only one thing. Those who resigned were the guilty ones, so they bowed out before they were fired. The second article was much more provocative in content. It was published Friday morning. It made sense, depending on who would be reading the article, however it appealed for public restraint and admonished the government not to take their patience for granted that they were not turning a blind eye. The writer sited as reference, the plight of the down trodden Peasants of Stony Gut and Morant Bay, who made a petition to the Queen of England to make some crown land available for them to cultivate but were refused. As a result, they were made to feel hopeless and helpless, because it was believed that the governor who was quite austere, influenced the Queen's decision. The writer, Mr. George William Gordon, namesake of a very public figure and advocate of the poor, pointed out that when the public was made to feel helpless and hopeless because they were under represented, and could not trust the government, they would resort to action like that of the people in Morant Bay who demonstrated their frustration. They lost their patience and took matters in their own hands and staged a huge Rebellion. Some of the elite farmers said Mr. Gordon, was provoking the public. Proactively though, he said he hoped that he would not suffer the same fate as George William Gordon, who was hanged for speaking out.

Cautiously, the government responded, in a newspaper article that the committee's report was due in Parliament in two days and would be made available to the public shortly after. They explained that the document was very large, and it took much time to get it done. However, the very next day the shocking news leaked and ran like wild fire over the country. At every corner of every street and lane in the capital, you could see people reading the news and the vendors riding bicycle ringing their bell to make another sale. This news was dispersed throughout the country. The headline read, "government caught with their pants down."

Chapter 7

Then the leaking of the story caused some people in the market place of ideas, to voice opinions that the leaking of the report was very timely. To them, it was possible that money had exchanged hands to get that report in the press at that opportune time. In their opinion, if it was delayed, some other hands of dishonest person in the government, would have exchange money and ideas to mislead the public. Therefore, said the layman of the opposing party, it was the best thing that could have happened to the country. Early that morning, the roving microphone crew returned to the streets to probe for answers on whether the public was pleased with the report and tried to find out how the article got into the papers before the government was ready. The headline read "Government caught napping."

While the document focused on many favorable aspects of child care, there were some that were disturbing. Critically, they showed up the government's inefficient policy of institutionalizing young children. Foster care placement was better for abused children and adolescents, which was the main method of caring for orphans and other needy children. The foster care program was preferred to the institutional style of management, and there was a call for the expansion of foster care and the downsizing of large institutions that were wasteful, costly and inefficient.

The public bemoaned the wasteful spending of paying large salaries to directors who sat in their offices and saw their ship taking in water and waiting for it to sink but didn't do anything about it. Foster care, on the other hand, would see children living in stable homes with families who operated normally.

Yet, there was more shocking news about child sexual abuse. When the public read this news, they said surely it would have never been published, if it was left to the discretion of the government. Over 7,245 children were alleged to have been sexually abused in the last four years the report said, and some in institution for children. These allegations raised serious questions. Why was the public not made aware of such atrocities? Then there was a threat thrown out to the reporter which says: "Informer fi dead." Clearly this was a cultural reaction that was trying to silence those who dare to report on child abuse."The report says while it was not clear if more children were becoming victims of sexual abuse, statistics from the Office of Children's Registry showed a massive spike in the number of reports received, with the figures jumping from 121 reported in 2007 to 2652 within one year.

Then, even more alarming, another report featured children exposed to violence. The report said that many children in that country were not protected, namely in their homes, schools and communities. Schools, which were once seen as safe havens, had been reported in the media, alleging that student-on-student violence, student-on- teacher, teacher-on-student, and community-on-school violence was widespread. The report presented several statistical facts that supported the argument on the necessity of minimizing the effects of violence on children and helping them to cope with the stress.

These reports added fuel to the already combustible charged spirit erupting in Lily's system. Calls to Lily's office to get her reaction was unfruitful. However, she now had proof, that she could make her demands and wishes known. She could call for changes in policy and ask for reform to the Children's Affairs program in the country. This, however, wasn't without difficulty because she was not a member of the political directorate, or an affiliate to the government or opposition in any way. Thus, she was like a voice crying in the wilderness: "Make straight the way of Children's Services." Now she had to find the best option to make her appeal. She chose to make petitions by seeking public response of signing the petition. Social media played a big role in the proceedings. This had a very big impact. Hundreds of people signed the petition in support the of reforming the Children's Services and to computerizing the records. This overwhelming response gave Lily further support on which she capitalized.

One of her advantages was that the knew Children's Affairs Chairperson needed to establish and carve out a name on the list of important folks herself. Strategically, it is one thing about one's climbing high up the corporate ladder in an organization or public office but quite another about the persons that climbed alongside him or her. What matters most however, was how many others he or she would have mentored or influenced to step up with them. This brought up the real examples of political leadership succession in the country. The leaders of both parties left the leadership in capable hands when they died, and each candidate went on to run the government for separate times. This could not have been done without careful mentoring o successors. One mentee led his Party for fourteen years. This was some leadership which the new Chairperson would like to emulate.

And so, with her initiative, Lily organized town hall meetings and invited her the leader of Children's Affairs to attend. This face to face forum created a very big impact. Many people were given opportunity to voice their opinion, thus making their input in the new policy for Children's affairs. Those whose voices were not heard took pride in being present during the discussions. This caused the new Chairperson of Children's Affairs to score big in the upscale ladder of public affairs. Her ratings jumped higher than many of her predecessors and other ministers of government her senior. But more than all, it won favor for Lily. She was invited to one of the exclusive formal parties they held at the time, in honour of one of their elder statesman. Consequently, this rating boosted her credit with her employer Steve and Steve as well.

They were highly proactive, and big business which knew that "the secret of success is to do common things uncommonly well," John D. Rockefeller. They knew that investing in employee engagement leads to profitability. They realized that engagement is crucial to competitive advantage said David Bilinsky and Laura Calloway in their article The Case for Investing in Employee Engagement.

Consequently, Steve and Steve embarked on a quest to fully engage their employees because they clearly anticipated the outcome of an invaluable rating on their client survey. The reality is that, the affirmation of client survey is directly proportionate to employee satisfaction and leadership of the year for any company. This would naturally result in public ratings and employment in litigation of big cases. Therefore, Steve and Steve embraced the fact that good judgment and careful planning were the key components of achieving their goal. They saw the outcome before achieving it.

As a result, they never want it to be said of them "I am commanded to love you, but I am not commanded to trust you." Jesus trusted God, not man because he knew what was in their heart (John 2:24). They didn't know what was in their client's and worker's hearts, but they trusted that making right decisions would bring favorable result. (2012) Dr. Keith Johnson "Trust is created when leaders make right decisions. Right decisions are like deposits in one's bank account.".

Hence, Steve and Steve clearly, had ulterior motives when they set out to cultivate a path that would lead to measuring the emotional and intellectual commitment that employees should demonstrate toward the firm. They realized that true leadership does not wait for destiny to show up; they receive it and then create it. Wherefore high employee engagement is certainly one factor that shows that an employer is rated highly by their employee.

Consequently, at the firm they implemented a social recognition initiative. They highly rated performance, loyalty and commitment. This placed Lily in a secure position. She was rated by the public, highly recognized by the government and now demonstrating a high level of leadership and integrity with her employer privately.

While demonstrating a public persona which portrayed her with Steve and Steve on the front page of the number one best seller, Leadership Quarterly Magazine she remains humble. Therefore (1) she achieved stardom in the infancy of her career. (2) Her potential magnified what she could be to the firm in the future.

One of the qualities of good leaders is that they never forget their past as a learning tool. The past will exchange position with destiny, but its wealth of experience is always available. Leaders of destiny are future focused. They look through the front windshield as they drive forward on the journey to making their dream come true, like Steve and Steve. Then, they ask tough questions and find realistic answers. (2012) Like Dr. Johnson. They asked intriguing questions: "Where are we going? When are we going to get there? What are we doing? Why are we doing it? Are we getting results? And what are we going to do when we get there?

As a result, they decided on a mission to reinvent themselves. Lily being a product of this new vision undertook the process of engaging in leadership training as always, she was striving to be the best she could. In the process, as a budding leader, she reflected on her purpose for going to law school. Her intention to practice law to be the voice of the voiceless, for young people who fell through the cracks like her mother, and use her business skills, to grow and manage her dad's business. As she reminisced over it, it became a beautiful affair. Just like in her valedictorian address at high school, she revealed her motivation for why she wanted to practice law and used her mother as an illustration. Hence, empowered by destiny she packed all her trophies, her accolades, and radiated the essence from her public persona and paid a surprise visit to Daddy that left him speechless for some minutes.

Lily had overcome her pride, the stress brought on by reading her mother's black book. She wished that her dad would lift her as he did when she was eight years old. Oh, how she longed to feel his arms around her and hear him call her those endearing names. But at the height of her statue, six feet tall, her wishes were impossible. Consequently, she set out to cultivate the atmosphere, to bring back memories of the past as close as it could get. After the shock, she insisted on calling him "My Daddy" and that he should call her his choice of childhood name that he was comfortable with. He chose to call her "Baby Girl"

Their features had changed somewhat. His head was no longer flushed with black hair, it was very low cut and showed signs of gray around his temples. His tall angular face was more leaned and clean shaven, but his brown eyes remained full and piercing. His tall six feet three inches angular body and broad shoulders remained muscular and strong. He was alert and jovial as the Daddy she knew. His brown hands were covered with gray hair.

He was surprised to see the changes in her features as well. She was a tall young woman, not quite as her father but, stately, upright and comely dressed. She had a distinguished head of natural hair combed just as her ninth -grade days braided, with a colorful band around her forehead to keep her braids in place. She wore blue jeans, shirt and pants over blue sneakers and tall blue socks with the feet of her pants tucked in them. She was still Daddy's girl but just grown up. For the first two days, all she did was reminisce on the past, and talk about the good times they had together. She thought it was prudent to reveal the secret that led to her break down as a teenager, yet she chose to leave it for the last. So, she turned her attention to the business of her visit. She set out to ask Daddy the important questions of destiny she learned in her leadership training.

"Where are we going? When are we going to get there? What are we doing? Why are we doing it? Are we getting results? What are we going to do when we get there?"

Daddy was baffled over these questions although she briefed him and gave him a copy of the agenda including the questions, to look over but he didn't take enough time to formulate reasonable answers. Certainly, he wasn't too clear in his responses. As a result, she helped him to turn his destiny and dream into a workable business plan. This gave her the opportunity to guide him in the path of destiny not just as a banana farmer but of his responsibility as a Kingdom Citizen. When she was finished, Jerry had a whole new perspective of his business and purpose.

So, as Jerry had seen the light, he invited all his workforce to a training seminar to be taught by Lily. Everybody was supplied with a blueprint of the new company's manifesto which was locked in a vault but was available on request. Also, each person got a tablet. Dave in addition to being driver had also become Vice President, to Jerry who was CEO, received a laptop. He, like everybody else, was expected to share in the responsibility of making the company successful. Some of the money that Jerry had stashed away in the bank was used to reinvent the company. Every worker was personally recognized for their contribution to the company. They were given new uniforms and promised pay raises when the company turned around.

Consequently, the whole attitude of Jerry's Banana Growers Association became a model for the All Island Banana Producers Association. Jerry didn't only see a new attitude in his workers, but soon began to see real profit, and true to his word he gave pay raise to all his workers. He was now the face seen on the new AIBGA's monthly magazine. He was also given a new role of Training Officer and advisor to the leadership of the organization.

Consequently, Dave was given more responsibility to manage the company in Jerry's absence. Dave had just turned forty and showing signs of gray hair around his temples and side burns. He had a distinguished spot of gray hair at the front of his head above his forehead. He had dark eyes and a gold tooth at the side of his mouth just below his left incisor that glistened whenever he smiled. Dave was amiable but business like and commanded respect from all the workers.

He did his job with much pride and efficiency. Jerry was always pleased with his leadership. Every Monday morning the workers arrived, he had a briefing report of what was accomplished the previous week and he congratulated his workers for a good job done. At the end of the month he gave out prepaid card to whoever distinguished him or herself during the four weeks.

Next, Lily turned her attention to re-establishing the reading competition that her dad started when she was a child. This time there was no one to accuse him of nepotism. The competition was bigger, better, and more widespread. It was opened not only to the citizens of Murton Town, but this time involved all the public libraries in the parish. While the format remained as her dad had originally advocated, the prizes were more valuable, so it attracted more interest and contestants. For this reason, she appointed a community to manage the contest and had her dad sit on the board as an ex- officio member.

Though he didn't have the power to vote on issues or make any decisions, she thought his ideas and experience would provide good insight into the activities of the board. Further, she recommended that he be designated in the bylaws as "ex-officio" so that it was understood that his role was very clear. He could serve only in an advisory capacity, while Lily remained CEO of the organization. So, she performed her duties as promised and returned to her position as a principled young lawyer in the criminal court. She now turned her attention to the case of representing those accused of criminal actions who were the public's sworn enemy.

However, her public persona and visibility in public square softened the response she got from the market place as she attempted to represent their number one enemy in court. She was aware of her self-esteem and knew that she didn't have to do anything extra to gain the public's trust. She wasn't just Lily, but Attorney at Law Lily Abigail Smith Parks. This case that involved two women and three men could either make or break her.

The lawyers saw the end of the case even before it went to trial. It was Lily's responsibility to research the case and find loopholes that would render doubts in the jury's mind so that they could find probably cause for dismissal. She must create reasonable doubts in the jury's mind. Her first duty was to categorize the charges into felonies or misdemeanors. But as far as the law was concerned, robbery, burglary, larceny and shooting with intent were felonies that needed no categorizing. They were what they were, nothing more and nothing less. Each involved serious misconduct that was punishable by law. Misdemeanors on the other hand, are conducts for which the law prescribes punishment of not more than one year in prison. These are such violations of road traffic and parking infractions. However, the charges in this case have far bigger consequences.

Parliament through the Ministry of Justice has the exclusive and inherent power to pass laws to prohibit and or punish criminals. These laws must be defined with certainty so that citizen and the court can understand them. Therefore, Lily had to prove her understanding of the people she represented. She must disprove two elements to create doubts that their clients were not guilty. These were overt criminal acts and criminal intent. In the first place, she must prove that their client, the defendants, didn't purposely and knowingly committed robbery, burglary, larceny and shooting with intent. Or it would mean they committed these acts willfully and purposely and at the time they were in their conscious mind. If so, they were reckless, knowing the risk and willfully disregarding it. Secondly, she must prove intent. For example: in the case of robbery, there must be evidence that they took things from the presence of someone by force. The criminal must show some intent before the act. On the other hand, the jury may infer that the so called, criminals had tools, such as sledge hammers or rocks that they used to break the windows. Their fingerprints would be found on these objects that they employed to break in and committed these acts. Yet, there were no tools present. Similarly, there must be a gun or guns and shell casings to indicate that they used such to commit the act of shooting with intent, but no such evidence existed. Consequently, Lily submitted her findings to her senior partners who in turn presented them to the court. Fortunately, for those they represented, the arresting officer blundered in the investigation. The Chief of Police gave the case to a subordinate officer who didn't get the facts right. The cop failed to advise the prisoners of their rights in custody. Plus, the officer questioned them without recording the interrogation. Hence the full report had misleading information. This was quite embarrassing for the Chief. As a result, the defendant's lawyer Steve and Steve called for a No Contest Submission and it was granted.

This was to spark a big protest. The five defendants had to be held into police protective custody. As for Lil, she came under the wrath of the public. She had been accused of being a traitor and the public showed their disgust. She had her four tires slashed, one day when she came out of her office. Another time she had graffiti written on her windscreen. Luckily, the perpetrators didn't mean to harm her physically, but they just had to vent their frustration physically and on Facebook. This only stopped when the full text of the case was published in the newspaper,and the subordinate officer was transferred to an unknown police station to practice law enforcement. As for the five offenders who got away free, they were never heard from again. Rumor had it that they all migrated to unknown countries. Therefore, Lily breathed a sigh of relief as she concentrated on her mission of advocating for the voiceless.

Consequently, her first response was to a case of suspected murder and extreme abuse of Tina, a 12-year-old child. She was missing for a few days but to most people she was missing for months. Some people said she was sick and the family was hiding her. Tina's body turned up after a unanimous caller reported a body of a child found in an abandoned house at the end of a cold sack on 15 Street in east central-township of the capital. The caller said the body was still in a good shape. The call was reported at 5.30 PM. The evening was hot and humid. The May month sun was setting but it had a marked effect on the temperature. It was 86 degrees, foreign height but felt like 100 because of the level of humidity. Lily wasted no time to get to the premises.

It was an abandoned, unfriendly, older building two houses from the end of the road overlooking a gully. There were the remains of a couple abandoned cars and garbage stocked higher than the average height of any man in that city. Surely it will roll over into the gully, any day if it wasn't collected quickly. The surrounding houses were in poorly kept condition. Paint stripped and faded colors, add to the dismal site. No one seemed to be around but as soon as Lily got out of her car about six little boys arrived on the scene and surrounded her car. If you lined them up, you could see them in descending order from four feet ten inches to three feet six inches tall. She hesitated a bit before stepping out in the street. She surely made an impression on the biggest boy who began to whisper to one of his group mate. He smiled and waved to her saying: "Hi Miss Lily, what brings you into this rough neighborhood?" He wore the most beautiful smile on his hardened face.

"Do I know you sir?" She replied to him. He looked more like 13 years old.

"Probly' not, but I know you." "You mean probably."

"Yes. You are the lady whose car those bad men wrote graffiti on," he said, in his pleasant voice. His hair was knotted but clean. His shoe seemed to be hand-me down, yet she really admired him. Although his shoe was bigger, much bigger than his feet he took pride in being clean. He didn't look like the others who were all bare upper body as well but dirty, except for one. This one seemed quite refined. He was wearing school uniform, but it was different from the Public-School student. He was clad in fine blue shirt and denim khaki pants. He wore brown shoes and socks to match his shirt.

"How did you know that?" she asked.

"Everybody knows it," the older boy said. She ignored his last comment. He kept his pants in place with his hands in his pocket. He wore clean T shirt. Speaking about Tina, he said that people said that she lived with her grandmother up the street, who is a 'paraplega.' "Paraplegic," she corrected him, but that's not true. Tina didn't like outdoors. For months, she hadn't been seen. "Did you hear about the missing girl?" "What missing girl?"

"It was over the news."

"Don't you call yourself the voice of the voiceless? How didn't you know about this girl who does not like to talk? It is the same girl, but they make it look like another, for she was missing for a long time. They said she lived with her grandmother but who could believe it. The girl lived with her Mother Miss. Punchy. Shelby Brown is her right name," or the red girl with auburn hair as Lily came to understand. She was a go-go dancer in night club that attracted many male clients but, she got caught in a drug raid and did time in prison. Few people believed that she could fall in such hard times. How could a smart girl like her allow herself to be so used? Her friend was to bail her out, but he had to take off and run for his life and has been hiding out in a foreign country ever since. She was independent of drug lords who set up her fiancé but the deal went sour and fell in her lap. During her vacation in the big house she met Loidie, after whom she patterned and dyed her hair.

Chapter 8

Loidie mister Dread, LD, with a capital D, was Lloyd Daniel. He was notorious for escaping from the police custody. He was tall, handsome, red face, and green eyes. He always wore his hair low cut, and in his hay days he wore tailor-made suits. Now that he was back from vacation too, he fell off shape his friends said. He got out of jail because he allowed all his assets to be frozen and he became the crowns witness in a huge drug bust. He went through rehabilitation training and was given the job to work at the doc. As far as the public knows he died in prison, but he went away for five years to some foreign country and was deported. Now he and Shelby are having good times together, but he has a cruel nature. "So, tell me more about this girl People say is missing three days." "That is not so. Her mother was on drug." the boy said.

One of the boys elbowed him, suggesting he was talking too much. The other boys suddenly started drifting away and one pulled on his friend's shirt to get him to leave.

"You never told me your name."

"Easton." The other boy tried to shut him up by attempting to cover his mouth. She got it though; he was Easton. The girl's name was Tina; she lived with her mother and stepfather. She had one sister who was missing as well.

As soon as the boys were out of sight she pushed the gate opened and went inside. The house had a foul smell. Nothing was in order but the contents around suggested that someone or more than one frequented the house. There were empty beer bottles and tins on a table. Foot prints were marked out in the dust on the floor.

Butts of marijuana and cigarette were strewn over the floor also. She pushed one of the doors looked inside and wheeled back outside and stood face to face with an unshaven man in his early forties. He was dressed in jeans, a half dirty white shirt and an oversize black jacket.

"Who are you?" the man demanded. "Who are you?" Lily fired back.

"You have no right here, you must leave," the man said.

Lily stood her ground and stared at the man. "Is this your house?

The man softened up. I never see you before." "Don't you put me out!"

"No, I won't put you out if you give me some information." "What information? Anything I'll tell you."

"Ok, let's start with your name, and where you have been for the past three nights? He straightened up. "My name is Alphonzo. I go to ST. Thomas to look for my cousin. She is in hospital. I get a ride. The bus wouldn't take me to go but it takes me to come back. See I have on clean clothes."

"What is your cousin's name?"

"Daisy, Daisy Dwyer, only she looks- out for me."She took out her cell phone and dialed a number. "Sonia, please fax me the number for St. Margaret's hospital." She got the fax and dialed the number. The phone rang but no one answered. What's your cousin's name again?" "Die, she has surgery. Daisy is my best cousin, I hope she makes it."

She dialed another number. This time it was the police.

"You are going lock me up?" The man turned and bolted through the door. Lily ran through the door after him. A police car was coming down the street. Alphanzo stopped and looked behind him.

There was nowhere to run. The impulse of turning back and jumping into the gully faded as quickly as it came. That would surely cause him bodily harm. So, he waited until the police vehicle was near to him. He made a dash past and continued running. One officer, a huge tall man, jumped out and pursued Alphanzo. Lily and the other officer watched until he caught up with him.

The other officer approached Lily and she accompanied him back into the house. "There is a homicide in this house," she said.

"Do you suspect that man?" The small, young looking officer asked. He was frail looking in body and his new uniform made him looked queer. He carried a new note pad in his hand that had never been written in.

"No." Lily answered. "Then why did he run?"

"Homeless people are afraid of police. They have been hurt so many times." "How did you find out about this case?"

"I got an anonymous call."

"Do you still have the number?"

"Sure, but it is classified. I cannot give it out. If the person wanted me to know his or her name, the message wouldn't have come from an anonymous source in the first place. Hence, I choose not to divulge this secret.

"You know that there are ways that I can employ to get you to cooperate."

"Who doesn't know that?"

"Well let me hope it will not come down to that." "To that what?"

"You know what that is, so I don't have to spell it out."

"Will you stop; stop behaving like an untrained..." She paused and looked at him. "By the way, how long are you on this job?"

He drew up his sleeve and looked at his watch. "Longer than you can imagine. Let me see 15 minutes."

Lily gazed in his eyes and said: "How long are you on the force?" He looked at his watch again. "One day and ten hours."

"So, you are a rookie. Well rookie," she paused for him to state his name.

"Douglas," he said.

"Well Mr. Douglas, don't get smart with me. Are you going to wait for your senior officer, or are you going to check the body until he comes?"

Before he replied senior officer Stone Wall J, came dragging what seemed to be the insane fugitive with him. Apparently, he had this rare mental imbalance that got him into a state of insanity whenever he encountered extreme force of the law.

"Don't you see the man is dying we need an ambulance." Lily reacted passionately. She dialed 999. As quick as I can remember, the big oversized ambulance came roaring down the street and brought with it two guys that provided much comic relief. They both jumped out of the truck and briskly walked through the open gate and door. As soon as one of the rescuers cast an eye on Alphanzo, he burst out laughing and turned to his fellow mate.

"Look who we have here."

"Come, come Fans," said the other. "We know your tricks."

"You boys stop it. You don't make fun at this poor man's calamity. You come joking over Alphonzo's dilemma, just get him some help." "'Dilemma,' she calls it 'dilemma'," as he chuckled. "This is routine for us," he said. We encounter Alphanzo at least once every week or two, sometimes once every three days. Tell her Fans, when last you went to St Thomas."

"He just returned today"

"So, what? He just returned today," Stone Wall joked.

At the sound of this assumed defense from Lily, Alphanzo straightened up, brushed off himself and managed a sheepish grin. "Don't believe them Miss Lily; they make up stories about me all the time." He wheeled his embarrassed self on his heels, showing his toes protruding through the front of the uppers and the sole of his sneakers.

"Not so fast Mister, we have unfinished business to do down the station. I am sure you can help us out," as he slapped cuffs on his wrist. Young officer Douglas opened the door leading to the dead body.

The others stepped in to view the remains of what seemed to be the body of a twelve-year-old child. "Well boys, you did not come in vain. Alphanzo is alright but you still have work to do."

Police Officer Stone wall watched as the rescuers did a preliminary examination of the body. She lay in a crumpled heap on an old mattress. He said to them, "She was killed within the last three to four days. She had bruises on her wrist, and neck." He lifted her dress. "No signs of rape," he said. There were marks of cigarette burn on her stomach. He recorded his findings and Douglas followed his example. But there was something strange about the body. It seemed that there was some chemical used on it. It had big whales, and blotches. Those marks were consistent with an allergic reaction of some sort. Apart from all the evidence the skin irritation was most fascinating to Lily. Although it might not have been the cause of death she had a keen eye for investigation and took an interest in it.

Stone Wall pushed Alphanzo into the room. "Have you ever seen this girl before?"

He became wild. His eyes bulged, and he trembled as he attempted to speak. He looked at Lily.

"It is alright; you don't have to speak to them," she said. "Any officer can ask questions, generally, but you do not have to answer. The law does not require you to answer or to supply any information, unless the officer gives you a legal reason for making such a request.

As I have witness he has not given you a reason. You aren't under arrest, for this crime, you should be entitled to go on your way when you clear up the situation with them down town. By the way, why does the officer place you in hand-cuff?"

"They say I witnessed a robbery and shooting." "Did you?"

"No, I was minding my business, so when I saw things were heating up I took off down the street to hide. The gun men drove around looking for me. I could see them from where I was hiding but they couldn't see me. I showed myself only when they were gone. The police attempted to arrest me but that was part of why I went off to St. Thomas for one week."

"You didn't tell me that when you told me you went to St.Thomas." "I didn't have to tell. You never asked me."

"Of course, Miss Lily," he had a smooth way of speaking. "Do I have to go with the police to the station?"

"Well they seem to want to investigate more about what they thought you saw. Is he under arrest?"

"Under arrest? He is being detained. If we do not detain this man, we can't guarantee that we'll ever see him before another two weeks." "Ok Mr. Smart Man, do you want me to accompany you down to the station or not? Well you have to tell me all I need to know." "Any way if you do not wish to answer questions, you are entitled to go on your way, but you may have to answer them in court. You can, however, agree to talk. It is up to you."

"But they won't let me go." The men from the mobile ambulance wrapped the body and removed it to their truck to be taken to the forensic laboratory for autopsy.

Somehow Lily had to put up with Alphonzo's behaviour because she realized that he could have valuable information. Therefore, she drove behind the police car to the station. Luckily, it was not crowded.

Hence, she sat with him during the interview. "No, no you have not read him his rights." So, officer Stone Wall briefed Alphonzo of his rights. He told him: "You have the right to remain silent. Anything you say can and will be used against you in a court of law. You have the right to speak to an attorney; and to have an attorney present during any questioning. If you cannot afford a lawyer, one will be provided for you at government expense. Do you understand that?" Alfphanzo shook his head.

"I don't want the government's lawyer. They only have the government's interest at heart."

"I don't think so Alphonzo, but you don't have to worry about one, you will have me in your corner. Be just truthful and honest."

"Yes, Miss Lily, I don't tell lies. Well, unless I am compelled to, to get me out of a problem. And today I do not need to tell any."

"So, did you see the men who fired the shot?"

"Don't answer that," she said. "He told you that when things started heating up, he took off down the street and hid."

"But he also said he could see the gun men," officer Stone Wall interrupted.

"Yes, but they were wearing masks," Alphanzo replied. "When did you return from St. Thomas?"

"Today."

"Have you ever seen the girl who was killed?"

"Don't answer that. We do not have conclusive evidence to say that she was killed. So, if you don't have any more questions for my client will you release him in my custody?"

"One thing more: please don't leave town without my permission." Lily and Alphanzo walked out together.

"Alright counselor."

"Good bye Mr. Stone Wall. When will the autopsy be performed?" "Your guess is as good as mine. These things take time but as soon as I hear something I will call you."

Lily gave him one of her business cards and left. Now she must find a place for Alphanzo to spend the night. Arrangement could always be made for him the next day but for the night it is crucial. She must be able to locate him early the next morning. She thought of his step mother's invitation, but he protested. She also thought of a homeless shelter east of where she lived. Therefore, she drove past her residence and dropped him off for the night, though he protested as well. He had a slight problem. He isn't a man for rules.

For him to spend the night, he had to strip and have a bath before going to the dining room for supper then going to bed. This was a very hard task but since he was going to get a hot meal he complied. He ate heartily, and then he retired to his room. Alphonso's bed was upstairs overlooking the south. The south represented the inner city which didn't pause for sleep until the wee hours of the morning. The activities seemed to be on a faraway screen. You could see the stop and go of traffic at the intersections; you could hear honking horns and see figures of people move about. Alphonzo sat at the foot of the bed by his window as he gazed toward the south. He couldn't make things out plainly. Yet, he could see enough to entertain himself until he fell backward on the coyer mattress and had a restless night.

Alphonzo always had weird dreams whenever he slept on a bed. Put him on a cardboard box or even a piece of sponge and he would be alright for the night. On his coyer mattress bed, he had several dreams that disturbed his sleep. In one of his dreams, he visited his grandfather in the country, suburbs in the hilly parish of Hanover. He arrived late in the afternoon and stopped on the way at a bar to get a drink. He got involved with some drunken men who talked trash about their family, women they had been with and of course, their most recent death and ghost story, the latest in the village. As far as Alphanzo knew, ghosts didn't exist in town because of all the bright lights but do so in districts like the one he visited at Miles Town, where many ghost stories abound. It so happened, that he over stayed because of the movie of comic relief. He got absorbed in the entertainment and night shadows fell and engulfed the community. Likewise, everything seemed so real, even the dead man was buried at the end of the same street on which his grandfather lived.

Alphonzo made his way into the dark until about five chains from his grandfather's house he encountered a tall man right in the middle of the unpaved dirt street. He made a sound that local folks called cleaning the throat, the supposed man never moved. He tried to go around him. Yet, he could swear that the man moved in the same direction. Alphonzo became brave and summoned his courage to fight off his would-be attacker. With bended knees and a wrestler's stance he lunged forward, grabbed him low down and tried to throw his victim, as he declared: "You insane Bastard, get out of my way," as he tried to throw his opponent off his feet as he saw in wrestling movies. But to his surprise the man turned out to be a metal water drum reinforced with a slab of concrete and over laid with tar that folks in the country used to store drinking water. It had a half -rolled sheet of galvanized zinc that would lead water into the drum when it rained. The drum was half full of water. The effort left Alphonzo with a slight muscle strain in his lower back, because that drum with its contents weighed more than one hundred pounds. With his loud sense of humor, he looked up and saw the twinkling stars above, but he said: "Devil you full of "trickery" you really planned this one."

He woke up and couldn't go back to sleep until near daylight. But as soon as he fell asleep, he heard the ringing of a bell and a man's voice called out "Rise and shine." Alphanzo opened his eyes rolled over on his stomach and fell asleep again. Within a few minutes, he heard a loud banging on his door and a voice threatened not to save breakfast for him. On hearing that, Alphanzo jumped to his feet and rushed out of the room. He was greeted by a tall nun dressed in purple robe and a burly man who was half her size. The man slapped a broom in his hand and gave him orders to sweep off the stairs and the walkway before breakfast. He looked at the sheer size of the nun, and of the man who stood beside her, took the broom squeezed it into his fist. He shuddered against the task he was faced with, and reluctantly went to work.

Lily went to pick him up at eight thirty am. He smelled much better than the day before. She opened the trunk of the car and gave him a box. In it were a suit of jeans, a shirt and a pair of sneakers.

Lily drove him to the abandoned house, picked the lock and let them- selves into the house to look for evidence. Alphanzo went into a room to change in to his new outfit, while Lily examined the room in which the body was found for extra evidence. She picked up some fallen hair, a piece of finger nail and what seemed to be two samples of blood. She also spotted finger prints on the door which she snapped with her camera. The best piece of evidence found was a pair of latex gloves and a pair of dirty overalls Alphanzo found in the room. When he finished changing he summoned Lily by snapping his fingers at her to look. On examination, she found spots of what resembled dry saliva or mucous dried and stuck together and folded in tissue paper in the overall pocket. She tore a piece and replaced the evidence for the police to find, so that she couldn't be accused of tampering with evidence. She embarked on a task of asking him some pertinent questions, whether the overalls belonged to him, did he dump the stuff in the room, and whether he knew the girl or not. Yes, he really had known the girl, but didn't dump the stuff in the room.

Chapter 9

Alphanzo corroborated the story of the youth she met when she first visited the abandoned house. The girl was Tina, and she lived with her mother and stepfather into a house further up the street They treated the child very badly. She didn't go to school often and she was always crying. She didn't talk much, but her crippled grandmother who lived next door to the house her daughter and mother of the child lived, supplied much needed information to fill that void. Tina was quite an abused child. She was abused both by her mother and stepfather. She was beaten and locked up in a room, when her mother was away. She slept at her grandmother's house sometimes. She was a very secretive child so, you couldn't get anything out of her.

She lived in fear of her mother who felt that she was standing in the way of herself and that worthless Loidie stepfather her grandmother said. Four or five days ago they packed and left without her. Her mother didn't work but her stepfather worked part time.

"Do you know where he worked?"

"I think I heard him say that he worked some place down the dock. His favourite time was when the medical ship docked in the port. He told me that he learned a lot and had access to speak to the doctors from different countries. He got his best tips on these ships as he helped around when these ships and large boats docked."

"Have you any idea where they could have gone? Do they have any relative out of town that they could go to?"

"Punchy has a sister in St. Thomas that is in the hospital. She is the best one. But she had to do surgery on her kidney, if you can find a man name Alphanzo, he is my step son, he can tell you more about her." When Alphonzo heard his name, he got up off the step and went inside.

"Speak of the devil and here he is," said Grandma; who sat in a wheelchair. She was quite old, somewhere north of eighty years. She had gray hair, and watery red eyes. But she had the most radiant smile. It was unusual to see an older lady with such a touch of humor and clear memory."Speak of the devil and here he comes." She folded a four- sided cloth, to reveal three ends and tied her head."Why don't you tell Miss Lily about Daisy? You know better than I because you visit her all the time even when she was in the hospital."

"Alright I will talk to him when you are finished." He withdrew himself so as not to encounter any of Lily's questions before grandma.

"So how old is your daughter?"

"Thirty-six. She is my only daughter alive, my other daughter died of kidney failure. Lord don't make Daisy die."

"So, you don't think Punchy could have gone there to see Daisy?" "Alphanzo, come in here. Him is so shifty, sometimes I cannot understand him. But it is not his fault. From he was beaten and abused by the police him just turn worthless, and' fraid, fraid'. Miss Lily wants to know if you think Punchy is gone to St. Thomas."

"I don't think so. I would have seen them. I just returned from there yesterday." "Thanks Mr. Alphanzo," said Lily to make things appear normal as if they never met. "I have to ask you one more question: Did you know that Tina died a few days ago?"

"No, no, don't tell me so. What kill her? Who kill her? Where is the body?"

"At the forensic lab, they are going to perform an autopsy to find out how she died."

"You sure about that Miss Lily," Alphanzo inveigled a cover up. Well if the police said so then we must believe them.""So, it is murder," the badly shaken elderly woman said. "Nothing but that worthless Loidie stepfather caused her death. He never liked my Tina," she said, at the point of tears. "And because of the dimness of my eyes I do not see so well. " This, drew compassion from Alphanzo and revealed another side of him. He went in her refrigerator for a bottle of water for the old lady and gave her hand towel to wipe her tears, though he didn't speak. He just patted her on the back and withdrew to a chair near the door. "Well Grandma I have taken up enough of your time, so I am going."

"Before I go I want you to know that you are a wonderful lady. I really appreciate the time you take to share with me. I will ask Alphanzo to come with me; I would like to talk to him about Daisy." "Alphanzo you must come back and sleep here tonight. You can sleep on the cardboard and sponge under the bed. Suddenly I am afraid."

"I will come back to see you soon Grandma that's a promise. You have keen memory and I love you for sharing your ideas." Lily said.

As soon as they were out of the house Lily snapped at Alphanzo. "So, tell me, what else are you hiding from me Alphanzo?"

He began to unbutton his shirt. "So, you think I am obligated to tell you everything you don't ask me?"

"Why are you taking off your shirt?"

"When I am in my own clothes, I don't have to put up with foolishness like this. Because you give me these clothes you think you own me. I answer to what you asked me. So, don't blame me for what you don't hear." She ignored his rash like two-year-old behaviour because little people who throw temper tantrums believe they are entitled to get their own way.

"So, Daisy isn't your cousin, she is your sort of step sister."

"If that is what you call her."

"What is Tina's mother right name?" "Punchy."

"Did you know that she was on drugs?"

"Of course. Both she and Loidie are on drugs." "So, do you take drugs too?"

"I may look stupid and sound stupid but that does not mean that I must act stupid."

"Do you think Loidie could have caused her death?"

"Now Miss Lily, are you sure that you are not treating me as the police?"

"No Alphanzo, I am your lawyer."

"My lawyer, what do I need a lawyer for?"

"Because I believe that you are mixed up in this whole mess. You began to lie from we met, you have lied to the police, it is only a matter of time before they come looking for you again. So, will you answer my question?"

"What is the question again?"

"Do you think Loidie could have caused Tina's death?"

"That man is quarrel. He burned her with cigarettes. He burned her stomach and another place she didn't want to show me."

"When was the last time you saw her?"

"Nearly two weeks before I went to St. Thomas, I visited grandma and she was present." "However, did you know that she was dead?" "You asked me that question already."

"I don't think so. Please refresh my memory." "No, for the second time."

"What was the occasion?"

"I glimpsed her looking out through the window one day last month. I waved to her and she drew the curtain."

"Was she with anyone?"

"She does not keep company, but how could I see if anybody was in the house with her?"

"I am going to the forensic lab and I want you to come with me." "Why?"

"Just shut up and get into the car Alphonzo." He complied.

At the lab, Alphanzo cooperated beautiful. He was a relative who was representing his crippled mother. Lily supplied him with all the questions to ask and he played along. The technician revealed the body and gave a brief report. "The cause of death is consistent with asphyxiation. She was strangled. Some bit of cord or rope was tied around her neck also her hands were tied. Whoever did this, hated her. There were marks of cigarette burn on her stomach and her buttocks. So, this person really wanted to hurt her. But there was something strange about her skin and her liver. There seemed to be evidence of poison. It seemed to react very slowly the coroner told me. Poison of that nature first affects the liver, then, it would be manifested on the skin.

Consequently, Lily requested custody of the body for burial. With no parent or relative with ability available, to assume the responsibility, the child would get a pauper's burial. The department responsible for poor relief gives assistance to families who cannot pay the cost associated with funeral give the equivalent of $250. A special part of the cemetery is reserved for this burial. Lily took the assistance but organized to give the child a decent burial. She appealed for donations and was frankly surprised at the response. Her motive was calculated however. She needed to get samples of her DNA tested to learn more about the poisoning. Therefore, after receiving specimens she arranged and had a worthwhile church burial in the public cemetery. She also reserved the rights to exhume the body should it become necessary.

Now she had the task of finding her killer because this would probably give a clue as to who administered the poison, if it was indeed poison. She took Alphanzo home to his stepmother's house and informed him not to leave town. She then returned to her office, after an exhausting day before heading home. She woke up in the night and couldn't sleep, so she lay awake and began to examine the case before writing a report for Steve and Steve. Suddenly, she realized that the case had grown bigger than she expected. She must find a lab to analyze the specimens, but she didn't want to use the local forensic lab.

She logged into her computer to look for the poison associated with symptoms presented. As a result, fortune smiled upon her. She discovered a product called Dioxin. It was published in the London press on 12/12/2004. It was the high- profile case in the Ukraine. A man named Victor Yushchenko was running for political office in Ukrainian government. It was alleged that another candidate intended to get him out of the way. When he was tested his blood, Dioxin was 1,000 times the upper limits that it should have been. However, if it was applied in very minute dose it remains in your body for a long time and slowly kills you. It means that whoever administered the small dose of Dioxin to the child or she ate contaminated food, meant to kill her slowly but suddenly thought it was taking too long and decided to strangle her. If Lily's theory is right when they apprehend the killer it would probably provide evidence about who tried to poison her.

Dioxin often produces abdominal pain problem with your liver and discoloration of the skin by lesions and blisters. Then she paused, realizing that it was a case of abuse and neglect and this must have been reported to the Children's Services. Therefore, she not only paid a visit to the office early next morning, but also to the children's hospital. The records showed that the child was admitted twice when signs of her symptoms were first appeared.

However, the parents withdrew her from that Children's hospital care and took her to another hospital. There she was treated, given prescription and sent home. A check with the local pharmacies suggested that the prescription had only one entry. The question was how could that child survive without the medication? This must have been a miracle. However, it was even more compelling for the Children's service to have intervened and rescued the child. This accounts for why she cried and locked herself away.

Although Lily reached the Children's service office at 9.am and the door opened at 8.30 the line stretched 200 persons long. The security officer on duty was exasperated that early in the day and was mopping perspiration from his face. Trying to control angry people who were there from all over the Cooperate Area waiting from 6.am was not an easy task. There were those who got there early, waiting in line to enter because it was first come, first serve. Some might not have had information as to the opening hours, but others didn't.

Lily was given special privilege to enter because of her status. She went inside to meet upon scores of people waiting. She shrugged her shoulder, and gave a dismissive wave of the hand, confirming the urgent need for action to change the services offered. The Social Worker, who supervised that morning shift, was busy, walking back and forth, calling names and directing those who answered, to different rooms. The line outside remained long because the reception hall was full. Lily called to the middle-aged woman; identified herself and asked for information about Tina. The Social worker was blank as to who this child was. She scrolled her computer files but could not find a record of her. Apparently, her name was recorded on an unprocessed, unfiled list. Her case was reported months ago but the department had been mandated to computerize the system, so the name Tina Rattigan, appeared only on the unrecorded list but was not attended to.

"Do you mean that nobody visited her home, made a phone call, nor bothered to take special interest as a priority, although the abuse was reported months before, including a report from the medical Practitioner of the Children's hospital?" In frustration, the Social worker Mrs. Reid said, "I am the only social worker on duty today." She turned her head away. "I have 200 cases," as she waved in frustration, the number of files held in her hand. "Some cases just fall through the cracks automatically."

"So, you are telling me, Tina fell through the cracks." Lily leaned forward. Mrs. Reid shuffled backward. "May I tell you something?"

The social worker said, "Go ahead," without looking at her, and the next sound she heard didn't even jar her mind, until Lily said: "Tena is dead. I'm investigating possible murder."

Upon hearing this, Mrs. Reid put down the files and looked at Lily. With trembling lips, she stammered, "When did she die?"

"I'm investigating the case. May I remind you that I don't have all the information. Before I call the police"

"So, what do you want me to do?"

"Well to start, you need to submit a report explaining when the case was reported; how many months ago?"

"Seven."

"Reported seven months ago and the child wasn' t visited nor picked up? That will take some good explaining to do." Mrs. Reid closed her eyes and massaged the back of her neck. She smacked her lips with her tongue. "I remember the Minister threatened to make heads roll," Lily added. The defiant social was overwhelmed by the news wheeled and walked away steeping briskly until the slamming door down the hallway confirmed her displeasure.

Lily didn't mean to be a silent thunder clap, but she was the one who advocated for these cases to be computerized, furthermore, the time to get the job done was very short. Yet, it didn't preclude a little initiative that could resolve the issue of finding and protecting the child. That shouldn't stop somebody from delegating that responsibility. To date, they had only input surnames starting from A to P. The time and apparent work load showed up the inefficiency of the system. It also revealed the underlining problem, of short staff, overworked, underpaid workers and a matter of failed leadership. This was unacceptable as to how child abuse was handled. Hence Lily still had work to do to persuade the new head of department to remedy these shortfalls as a matter of urgency. Satisfied, that she addressed the issues, she then drove to her office to compile her report.

The official coroner's report came, as no shock but as was reported earlier, death was caused by strangulation but also suggested doubts about poisoning. The senior partner of Steve and Steve received and reviewed the report. He paid compliments to her for her initiative and detailed report but suggested that she visit Daisy and take Alphanzo with her. Officer Stone Wall through the initiative of his office launched an official man hunt to bring in Punchy and Loidie, who were prime suspects in the murder. When Lily visited Daisy in the hospital, she linked up with the police to find the suspects who had visited the sick sister a few days before. It was firmly believed that they were hiding somewhere in that town after someone reported that he saw two people in an older model car, fitting their description.

Checks were made at every motel, hotel and places of lodging but all turned out to be unsatisfactory news about the suspects. To emphasize the seriousness of the cause of locating the suspects Lily told Daisy more about the case. She needed to be aware, because if the suspects were aware that she knew about the case, they might try to silence her by killing her. With this intention, security was posted at the door 24 /7, as the man hunt continued.

Back home,Lily urgently took the samples from the lab,to her alma mater's research laboratory for analysis. The samples were consistent with evidence of Dioxin poisoning. With this information, Lily formulated a theory that the poison must have come from a foreign country, but how? She subsequently investigated all the government laboratories and pharmacies and private industrial companies but found no lead to the drug, being imported or locally manufactured. Then she hazarded a guess. Suppose the drug came in illegally. If so, for what purpose? To follow this up, she made an appointment with one of her senior partners to discuss her hunch and her findings.

Hence, she tabled her report. Dioxin is waste product of various industrial chemical processes and is highly toxic. Illegal levels of

Dioxin showed up in cancer causing drug in 8 % of food and feed samples taken from Europe in 1999 and 2008. What if the chemical was still at large; and animal products from these countries were brought into the island? If animal and fish oil products were or have been imported, or smuggled in, the possibility exists that when Loidie worked on medical, or commercial merchant ships, he could have got contaminated product or got contaminated himself. All these questions could only be answered when Loidie was picked up.

These animal and fish feed had the highest concentrations of Dioxin poison. The industrial substances were incinerated in forest fires and were deposited airborne on plants and water ways and enter the food chain. When ingested by animals it caused contamination of animal product. In recent years, health scares in Europe linked Dioxin contamination in foods that have included Italian buffalo, mozzarella cheese and Italian pork. Is there a possibility that Italian ships serve Italian quiescence made with mozzarella cheese in our port, and the contamination escaped?

"This was useful information,"said her senior, Jonathan Steve,"and will go a long way in solving this murder but they are mostly theories and conjectures; remember I say mostly. I have done some research myself. I discovered that a shipment of mozzarella was dumped a few months ago. Private companies don't just dump products like that unless something is really at stake. This shipment was in the works from last year when an Italian cruise ship made an impromptu landing in our doc last spring when the businessmen met and made the deal for the shipment. You must remember that such shipment would be heavily insured. Could this be motive for dumping, part or the whole? The question is," continued Steve, "was it dumped for the insurance or was it contaminated?"

"Your guess is as good as mine," said Lily.

"Ok," said Steve. "We need to formulate a bold plan and we need to act with urgency. I will have to get your whole team involved. To that end, somebody needs to be in St. Thomas. As soon as they pick up the suspects, this is critical to the case. Somebody must see that they are read their rights and they must shut up. They must request a lawyer. So, we must meet them at the Central police station, to monitor the interview," said Jonathan. "Which two of your girls can do that?"

She shrugged her shoulder. "I will delegate the responsibility," Lily said."Secondly, I will go to the company that dumped the cheese. This is going to be a very untouchable subject; therefore, I prefer not to put any of you in arms way. Then you will need to follow up with the Italian tour guide team who accompanied the passengers on the tour. You also need to find out if Italian farmers have experienced Dioxin poison lately."

Therefore, they were all given assignments with deadlines, except those going to St. Thomas.

"Thirdly you need to dig up everything about the tour, meal preparation, meals that involve milk and cheese, even the private whereabouts of guests. Then report to the station to stand in beside the suspects. We cannot afford for the police to interrogate them without your representation." So, it happened that Lily boarded a plane bound for Italy.

Each team went their separate ways. Going to St. Thomas was probably the easiest thing to do. All they had to do was to wait around until the suspect was apprehended even if it took many days. They had to book themselves into a motel overlooking the hospital, as not to miss any of the action so, they didn't sleep at the same time, but on shifts. While one slept, the other kept watch. They assumed that the suspects would show up at the hospital to see Daisy. It didn't take long before this scheme worked. However, not before they allowed them to slip through their hands a couple of times. A woman came to visit Daisy one morning early, dressed like a nun. She brought soup and flowers for her. Unfortunately, in the end when they were captured they learned that the nun was only Punchy, in disguise. Similarly, Loidie visited as an air-condition technician. The heat was so unbearable that the staff would allow anyone to come in and operate under a pseudo name. Again, this was disclosed when both were in custody. Jason Steve went to the station to represent Steve and Steve and to see that the suspects were well represented since Lily didn't return on time.

Next, Jonathan had promised to visit the company that dumped the cheese. Since he thought that it could be dangerous, he decided to go himself, armed with his licensed revolver. On arrival he was met by tight security. He had to sign in, showed his ID and calls were made to verify his identity, plus he had to surrender his revolver and was escorted around. He had to promise not to touch anything.

At first the company denied that the shipment did take place. Secondly, they didn't call the disposure of the shipment dumping, it was recycling. They recycled the shipment as a precaution because they suspected that it was contaminated but refused to disclose what the contaminants were. When they were asked how they recycled the shipment the manager shrugged his shoulder and said, "That is also classified secret as well."

Then came the real important question of the cost of the shipment which was $250,000, was insured for $350,000. The company speculated that storage would be a problem and sale of the product would take a very long time before they realize a profit. Therefore, instead of trying to store it to sell and fearing spoilage, they get rid of the stuff and collected the insurance and no one from the government institution bothered to investigate it.

However, as far as public response was concerned, the company was absolved of any responsibility that would arise. Hence, the company was guilty not of charges of causing contamination but insurance fraud. Why was the law that involved contamination of the environment not thrown at them? She wondered now, if there was some collusion and money exchanged hands. Again, how a product be insured $100000 more than its actual value? Was this a direct oversight by the insurance company? Or fraudulent transaction.

Consequently, Lily had to give her report with no conclusive evidence. She had a fact finding visit to Italy. It produced an interesting documentary provided by the tour guides. It summarized the results of cultural exchange, of an ongoing Cultural Revolution which was taking place between the two countries but failed to shed much light on the poison.

In Italy, she visited large farms where thousands of cattle were raised, she also had interviews with officials of certain provincial office. There was Mutual Corporation between the two countries which exchange recipes and food samplings as well as participating in dancing, crafts and visual arts but nothing about Dixon. Most importantly there was a two-year student exchange program worked out with the Ministry of Sports and Culture. However, there was a glimpse of hope in the whole affair. The sampling of food brought suspicion to the limelight. Lily's quest was to discover if Loidie sampled any of their food and if he took home any. This suspicion loomed big in Lily's mind. Therefore, she headed for Loidie's refrigerator to find clues. She found cheese, but it was a good thing she had kept it silent because it turned out to be false news. She had to find Loidie immediately to have an interview with him. Sure enough, Loidie did eat and bring home food for his family, but it wasn't cheese or milk base. He took home samples of his native food. He was given a souvenir CD of the two day's extravaganza. As a result, this absolved the tour company and the Italian connection of the dioxin poisoning.

Yet armed with a warrant they re-searched' Loidie's and Punchy's kitchen cupboard. That revealed the suspected culprit. Packs of Italian Mozzarella di Buffalo, also known as 'buffalo mozzarella', made from domesticated water buffalo milk cheese unopened. This got Lily real excited to find what she thought was a direct lead to this mystery. Therefore, she quickly took a sample to the lab at her alma mater again for analysis, but like others, it turned up negative.

Chapter 10

Now the defense team was left in a dilemma because the court date was set, and they didn't have a theory on which to base their case. They expected to be named company of the year according to the latest customer survey, therefore they couldn't go down as defeated because of some oversight. Hence, the partners met for a debriefing and brainstorming session which lasted three hours. Lunch was put off all telephone calls were put on hold, to be attended to at the end of the business day.

One thing they all decided upon from the outset was that the case was very complicated thus they were not at all alarmed by all the twisting and turning.

They examined it from various angles. They ruled out the Italian connection which they feel, bears no relevance whatever, samples of food were local, but they still had reservation about the dumping. The cultural exchange program was not a suspect. The so called recycled shipment of cheese left one question unanswered. The company didn't disclose what contaminants they suspected, and that Jonathan hoped to exploit.

He therefore got a subpoena and drove to the company to talk to management again.

This time they threw up their hand in the air and complained of harassment. But he had more cooperation and had his expectations met. This sent off palpitation in his chest. He calmed himself and learned that there was an outbreak of Dioxin poisoning in Europe, specifically the destination from which the shipment came. And although it was subjected to meticulous screening and analysis his shipment was not to be suspected of contamination, but they didn't prepare to take any chance.

Consequently, Jonathan needed to know who supervised the disposal or recycling as it was called. He had to know if all the shipment came in bulk or in separate compartment in different vessels. It turned out that the scientist who made the disclosure, was not affiliated with the company anymore and there was no forwarding address to seek his where about. Jonathan therefore got duplicated records of the transaction to used.

Consequently, the discovery was shocking. The scientist opposed the way the company went about the disposal. He believed the safest way to rid of the environmental threat was to burn it under controlled conditions, but the company wished to bury it. He engaged management about the danger of contaminating the underground aquifer, but he could not come to an agreement with management, so, he resigned and left the company. However, not before he made a video of the proceedings because he knew it would surface again.

Management was only careful about receiving the insurance which would benefit him in his bonus check, but he refused and walked away. Steve's task was to get a hold of this scientist whom he learned was abroad on vacation. Hence, Lily looked at, the possibility of speaking to different airlines to get a record of his travel an itinerary. The scientist Abernathy Gerard of Indian origin didn't return to India for vacation but instead went to the Bahamas. Lily's chest rose and fell as her heart pounded she moved through customs and sought permission to become the SOS, to seek him out.

It was easy to get his cooperation because she got a subpoena and all necessary papers for extradition if necessary. Henceforth, he turned over the video in lieu of him leaving his vacation to attend court. Back home, they prepared to go to the trial. The possibility also existed that some of the contents of the shipment found their way in black market and was being sold on the street and in corner stores cheaply.

So, after watching the video the attorneys were convinced that they could solve the mystery of Dixon poisoning. Lily spearheaded a call to ministry of health to launch a public campaign to sensitize the public of the danger of buying and eating Mozzarella cheese from street vendors and in corner stores. It so happened, that the mother and stepdad of the deceased child, were accused of poisoning the child. The story said they found out that the poisoning was guaranteed but was taking too long, therefore, one or both strangled the girl. But no evidence came to light to prove the case. No evidence of fingerprint or DNA showed any relevance. The overall found in the room, next to where the girl died was there for more than one year when the owner tried to do repairs on the building. The fingerprints Lily picked up didn't match or corroborated with the case.

Then the packages of mozzarella cheese were bought on black market but showed no contaminants. So, the parents were charged for obstructing justice by taking off to St. Thomas when they should have been present,to answer questions. They objected to the unsubstantiated charges, because, neither the mother nor stepdad could give any logical explanation as to why the girl was not in foster care when the recommendation was made by the chief Medical Officer of the Children's hospital.

The Department of Children and Family should have picked up the child several weeks ago. Both parents neglected their duty of insisting that the authority act accordingly. Plus, they both denied burning her with cigarette. To this Alphonzo's witness in court caused laughter that the girl showed him the burn on her stomach but not the other part of her anatomy. He was asked why he didn't report it to the police. He responded to this with his own question.

He raised his hand like a schoolboy caught in the act of doing something wrong. Everybody looked at him with keen interest to hear his stupidity. He addressed the officer: If you were a homeless person and made such a report, had such a record of encounter with the police, w ouldn't you be arrested on the spot for child molestation? Imagine then, if I had reported to officer Stone Wall that I knew this girl who told me that, would you immediately arrest me for specious child molestation? So, with this line of thought Alphonzo retorted: "I may look stupid and sound stupid, but I am no fool." Punchy was charged with three counts of negligence and abused and Loidie was charged as an accomplice. They were given time in prison, the mother one year and the stepdad nine months.

Yet, there was no breakthrough in the murder trial until there were three similar deaths, all girls, and ages twelve to thirteen years old. Each victim had cigarette burn marks and appeared to have been strangled. They had similar bruises around the neck and wrist. All of them had lesion no their skin, including blisters. Each girl was a loner, didn't talk much and was withdrawn. Which means that they had been selected by choice. One girl was resident in a foster home, the others lived with either step father and mother or single parent, working mothers. It happened that the children all started out with stomach pain that caused their parent to seek help at the nearest hospital.

The heart wrenching news broke when one of the leading news-paper headline the story: Strange Disease Outbreak. Four of the children were dead, seven were in hospital fighting for their lives. This buzz caught the attention of all the news media both foreign and locally. Most cases were being dealt with at the Children's Hospital. In the words of the Chief Medical Officer, "we have no reference of pass cases. We have never seen the likes of this disease." At this point, Lily and Jonathan, were obligated to come forward with their findings. This brought much publicity to the story. It was no longer lawyer and client privilege but a national crisis. This was when the Government decided to take a stand by allowing more law enforcement officers to start their investigation. After the first wave of reported cases, other incidents of the disease came trickling in but not as severe.

Consequently, the whole news of Dioxin Poison was presented as a documentary which got much traction not only locally but in Europe. It traced the disease from 2007 to the present, from the poison of Victor Yushchenko, to the outbreak of Dioxin poisoning in Italian food packages and the contamination of animal product to the outbreak in the country of the Caribbean. All of Steve and Steve staff members were interviewed by law enforcement officers, to bring deeper exposure to the crisis. It was then one parent came forward and reported that she was paid one hundred dollars to have her daughter participate in a survey to test the effectiveness of the wonder drug called Doxinate. Each of one hundred children were administered the drug in the first phase. A straw like tube was dipped in the drug and wiped on each child's tongue. It was assumed that if it was administered in very minute quantity it would disguise the potency, and not affect the children so quickly. This should have been repeated after nine months. All this should have been a secret but after three months the reaction to the drug was shocking.

The drug didn't only show up in Tina's body but affected some other children as well. This was part of what seemed to have been what Abernathy Gerard opposed, why he was relieved of his job at the lab. Steve and Steve turned over a copy of the video to the police but reserved the right as a Law firm for its use as defense tool. However, before the story broke the company which remained nameless because of litigation matters, laid off its staff and shut down its operation. When a journalist visited the company in the industrial belt of the metropolis, the gate was under lock and keys. A sign posted on the wall read. "This Company ceases to operate here."

Hence there was great concern as to the where about of the managers of the company. A reward of $50,000 was offered for information that would lead to the arrest of the perpetrators. If the authorities could locate the management, they could find out who was behind the experiment. Like locating Abernathy Gerard earlier, Lily stepped on the gas. She wasted little time in calling on the airlines to see if the managers left the island. In her anxiety, she didn't get the proper identity of those who were running the company. Therefore, she had to back track her steps and went to the Ministry of Industry and Commerce which had a registry of all companies and names of their management staff. There she found the Company's name to be Barclay's Food and Beverage, Old Sale and Retail. The owner and CEO lived in the Bahamas where he was managed the headquarters of the affiliate company. It was for that reason that Mr. Abernathy Gerard took his vacation and went to the Bahamas, to convince the CEO, to give him the job as manager of the local company. The video he hoped would support his claim to show that things weren't alright at the company. Since things weren't going well and the video would speak for itself. He had no idea that the company ceased operation, until he saw the news on television. As a result, he lost credibility of making a pitch for the new job. The local managers were scattered abroad between Atlanta Georgia, Los Angles and New York.

Locating them was a matter of urgency. Lily and her two partners armed themselves with subpoena and extradition papers and each dispatched themselves to the three states to bring back their capture. Photographs supplied by the Ministry of Industry and Commerce proved to be very helpful in providing proof of identity. Each manager, booked into an unpopular and unfamiliar hotel. One, for example, catered only for special high- profile Business Men. When you call the hotel for a business man by name, the security took you through rigid check- up, no doubt, to discourage potential whistle blowers or trouble makers. Then, when you have finished declaring your name and identity, you were interviewed by the business man's security. They demand to know, from what company or business you operate. If you were a tourist, you got utmost respect. All this was done to protect the identity of their clients. Each person would register under false company's name to cover their identity. However, with photographs, subpoena and the media attention they risked being exposed, so quickly cooperated and the managers received their papers forthwith and returned home to stand trial. With the lawyers approach it was totally impossible for them to deny. Given the help of local authorities, they were apprehended, held in protective custody and transported home to face the court. Somehow the news leaked out and there was a newspaper release with the headline: "Breakthrough in Dioxin Poisoning." And the story went viral. In one day, there were more than a million tweets.

The article named the company at which the managers worked and stated the day and time when they were expected to return from abroad. As a result, there was a mob of people waiting at the airport to get first-hand look at them as well as journalists who waited to get information for their newspaper column. Luckily, the law enforcement act proactively and set up barricades to prevent the public from getting near to them. Although their landing times were different, it didn't diminish the enthusiasm of the curious onlookers. Each was whisk away in unmarked police vehicles. There was a similar crowd of curious folks at the police station awaiting their arrival.

Unfortunately, Steve and Steve got the fifty thousand dollars that was more than their expense to bring home the accuse but they weren't allowed to represent them as their attorney. That the judge said would be a conflict of interest. They were represented by Cooper and Lions, who hired Lily to supply research evidence, since she had relevant information on the case, but she couldn't go into the court room.

Consequently, she submitted a report about Dioxin as she did to her senior partners. She explained that it was a waste product of various industrial chemical processes and was highly toxic. Next, she reported on the Illegal levels of Dioxin showed up in cancer causing drug in 8%. She also explained that the industrial substances were incinerated or burned, in forest fires and were deposited airborne on natural food chains such as plants and water ways. When ingested by animals they caused contamination of their meat and milk product. Next her report focused on the closing of Barclay's Food and Beverage/ Old Sale and Retail. It explained the situation why Abernethy Gerard gave up his job, and went on vacation in the Bahamas, the video he had made and the extradition of the managers who hurriedly left and went abroad. Also, the black market selling of mozzarella cheese and the suspects who might have been involved in the experiment.

The case went on for weeks. Representative of Cooper and Lions attorneys at Law tried to hammer out a case of no contest. Their case seemed solid until the video was brought in as evidence by the prosecutor. They objected to the video but when they heard that Mr. Abernethy submitted the video in lieu of him being present to testify, they rested their case. The three managers were charged for endangering the environment, thus the lives of citizens, by burying the shipment of contaminated cheese and were ordered to excavate it and dispose it by burning it under controlled condition in thirty-one days, as Mr. Abernethy suggested. The judge reprimanded the managers. He told them that they may not be able to choose what happens in the environment, whether it is sunny. Rainy, cold or hot but we can choose how we respond yo it. We may need an umbrella to keep out of the sun and rain, but we may not pollute it. They were also charged for ordering the use of an illegal substance for medical purpose also for operating medical experiment without a license that endanger the life of innocent children. Likewise, they were charged with conspiracy to commit murder. "The CEO of Barclay's Food and Beverage/ Old Sale and Retail" was charge with liable because it all happened in his company. Each manager was sentence to, life in prison. This didn't go well with the public which felt that they should get the death penalty.

As the proceedings continued officer Stone Wall Jackson testified to the court that from his investigation, Mr. Bygrave wasn't a real pharmacist. He had a license that permitted him to dispense homemade natural remedies, as well as a limited amount of over the counter drugs. Mr. Bygrave told of the meeting which he had with the three men in the back of his shop after closing hours to the public one year ago. They carried out the research of selecting and paying the parents of the victims. They also set up the appointments so that the victims came to his shop directly, after closing time, for him to administer the drug. He had no idea that the drug was illegal, or so dangerous. But he was promised a big reward when the drug got on the market. The two men got their information from an online source which was promoting the drug, as cure for childhood disease of every kind. The prospect of being rich was more powerful than to make use of commonsense. Hearing this disclosure, Bygrave was charged with twenty-five counts of administering an illegal drug and four counts of murder.

This phase of the proceeding took another unusual turn. He refused to be charged alone, so Mr. Bygrave blew the lid off the conspiracy theory in a passionate plea to the jury, that the killing by attempted strangling was Mr. Abernathy's idea. He paid him $30,000 to make the killing look like murder, so, the cord wrapped around the necks and wrist of the victims and chafe their skin was a fake. In turn, he paid step dads to wrap the cord around the victims. That was clearly the reason for Loidie and Punchy to pack their things and went off to St. Thomas because they didn't want to get more involved.

Each child died by an overdose not by strangling. This burst the case wide open. Abernathy's idea was that the faster the victims died the more powerful would be his case to get the managerial job and he would help Mr. Bygrave to expand his falling business.

This brought in the action of Officer Stone Wall and Lily to visit the Bahamas to bring home Mr. Abernathy to face the wrath of the court. He was charge for Aiding and abetting. In this case, he aided Mr. Bygrave in committing murder, and administering the illegal drug. As a result, Bygrave was charged with murder but had his sentence commuted to life in prison because he cooperated with the court in bringing down Mr. Abernathy, who was charged with conspiracy to commit murder and dispensing an illegal substance to the public. They like the other managers were remanded in custody their pass ports were confiscated and revoked by the court. The case was adjourned. Sentencing was set to commence on an indefinite date.

At age 25 Lily achieved most of the things she set her heart on doing. Yet, she yearned to fulfill her biggest quest, the one that dodge her mother for the better part of her child bearing years. Other things always seemed to take priority over her personal life. However, this would be her crowning achievement and a most interesting adventure. Well, to be wooed by a prospective husband and become a mother is a dream worth fulfilling. Yet, helping people was always first on her agenda. So, first she must get a hold of Alphonzo. She felt compelled to see him settled in an acceptable living condition, even if it was temporary. She placed her hand akimbo. She paced the office floor. She folded her hands. She scratched her nose then snapped her fingers. Yes, she got a plan. She looked at her watch. I must find Alphonzo. She was compelled by her conviction and she accepted the challenge.

Now she must find him. She raised her chin and braced herself for the night's adventure. She moved into action. She caught up with him. The night was cold. He was unfolding his cardboard mat for it was time to shield himself from the cold. She nodded to him. He drew a deep breath. He was quite surprised to see her. He wasn't expecting to see the likes of her. No, and not that time of night, in that area. "Hi Alphonzo, how are you?" He gasped. What have I done now you come looking for me? How did you know where to find me?" Who told you where I would be?""Well I know that you haven't been sleeping in the abandoned house anymore, so I did a little research, talk to a couple folks and here I am." She spread wide her arms in supporting her find. Alphonzo looked away but acknowledged her presence.

Suppose we go to the all- night restaurant, so that we could talk. She inclined her head in the direction of the restaurant. First, I must tell you that you are a promising and intelligent. You aren't achieving your God given potential. I really admire your drive to succeed even when the odds are stock against you. You have this remarkable way of ignoring stuff that would upset others in your position. So, you are the most outpouring success of those I represent. How about it? Will you come? I have a proposal for you." Proposal? He stood up and straightened himself. He cocked his head in unbelief. "Is that to get me back into that dingy homeless shelter?" he asked. I don't want to go back there. They have a Nun there who is as big as two big men put together. Then she has a body guard who looks mean and menacing like a trained bulldog and almost as big as her. They came banging on my door just when I was about to get my morning rest. They didn't only shove a broom in my hand; to go out and work but threatened not to give me breakfast if I didn't. Alphonzo held out his arms, to stop her from speaking.

When I live by myself I don't have to bathe or work on other people's terms." Yet, with reluctance, he finished rolling up his cardboard mat and stock it in a corner under a vendor's stall. She jerked her head in the direction to the restaurant again. He shrugged his shoulder in response and followed her closely.

He was pleased with how he was dressed although he hadn't taken a bath for some time. He was shaven and his jeans, the one Lily had bought for him was dirty but fitted him well. He wore a black jacket over them. He conjured up in his mind the kind of meal he wanted, a roasted duck, conch soup and a bottle of Heineken bear would do him right, then a complementary Cuban cigar though he didn't smoke. Since he wasn't paying for it, he might as well make the best use of the occasion. You wonder what the late- night folks thought about the scene of this bomb and his refined admirable companion. They walked inside. Furtive whispers, challenging gazes and flirting glances followed them to their seat. However, it all turned out that those who admired her did so from afar. Was she mixed up in drugs? they wondered. Alphonzo was special. He got his wish and Lily drank a cup of coffee and had a bowl of ice cream.

Chapter 11

"So, what proposal have you for me?" He braced his chest out to hear the good news. Feeling elated, he gesticulated with his arm revealing the sleeve of his dirty white shirt. "Well psychology was not one of my best subjects though I scored an A on that course. But one thing I have learned is that you can improve a person's condition by changing his environment or change their approach to doing things. I love the former because it is difficult to bend a tree when it is fully grown and knowing your stubbornness, I would not attempt to change your ways. Alphonzo adjusted the lapel of his jacket. I'm glad you're not trying to change me, because I wouldn't want to disappoint you" he responded. However, I believe that if you change one's environment, Lily continued, the impact in the right condition will nudge you individually toward changing your lifestyle."

"That is a beautiful speech Miss. Lily but what does that have to do with me?""Everything. I really thing you are a good man. You just need a little guidance. This town is hazardous to rehabilitation and recovery. You are going to meet the same friends who behave like you and continue in the lifestyle that got you in this mess in the first place. I heard that you were a fine mechanic once. Alphonzo brightened up, but dropped his shoulder limply, when he heard the rest of the speech. "Until you had that encounter with the police. Why did you resist? Didn't know my rights?" "Well I was younger and stronger I was more brawn than brain, stupid you may say."

"Any -way, the years you spent in jail are gone but you can reinvent yourself. You just need to take the first step. Every step you take is an important milestone on your new journey. Every move you make is crucial but the first step you take is most important because all the others are predicated on your taking this lone step. If you take the first step, that you must, in a positive way, you will get to your destination." Henry Ford said, "The whole secret of a successful life is to find out what it is one's destiny to do and then do it." "So, let those years be sacred. Let them be your teacher – let them be the voice of reasoning that will galvanize your wayward thoughts. When insanity challenges and seeks to control your thoughts, remember that you have greatness in you. Dave Gambrill says: you should Give yourself permission to step into your greatness." And Booker T Washington wants people to Judge you not by what you accomplish, but what you had to overcome for your accomplishment. "Take a moment and think of where you are coming from. Were you expecting to be sitting and having this conversation?" "No, not really" "Well this is the beginning of greatness in your profile. Never put down yourself."

"So, why all the big speech Miss Lily? I'm not one of those intellectual lawyers that you face in your meetings daily. Just tell me what you got to say, in plain words what is your proposal." Well I would like you to do is to change your environment and I have two suggestions. You can go out of town to The Rescue Mission or you can go to work with my dad on his plantation where he grows bananas." "What is the advantage of both?" He asked. "If I do take up your offer."

"Well, the Mission is a Christian place. It is called "The Rescue" because it helps to rescue people like you,those on drugs,unwholesome lifestyle and crime and violence. At the same time, it teaches people about themselves. For example, how to act in social settings, also they learn about Jesus and how to be a Christian. In addition, when you begin you do not come out to mingle with the public for a set period of weeks. You go to classes in the days and you study for the GED exam. If you do well, they find you a job. You will go to church on Sundays or Saturdays whichever you choose. "And the second?" If not, you can work with my dad on his banana plantation. You do anything the supervisor asks you to do. Whether you prune bananas, cut trenches, carry bananas, to the truck or to pack up the truck with supplies in the town. More than all, you don't pay rent from your pay check. One thing is asked of you is that you open a savings account at the bank.

You are free to go to church whenever day you choose. You won't be stuck inside the farm for anytime. You will make your own decisions and make the best of life as you see fit. Surprisingly Alphonzo sat up and crossed his legs. He brushed dust off his jacket that was not there. He cleaned his throat. Then he chose to go to the mission. He imagined himself passing the GED exam and getting a job. He could go back to be a Mechanic with a good company, then open his own business one day. He smiled broadly at the prospect of being his own boss. However, he conceded, that if he had to cease mingling with the public, to change his lifestyle like wearing clean clothes and taking a bath regularly, it would be worth it.

Therefore, that was settled. This was a very smart choice that he made, in that he would have an all-round more productive life. He would get a chance to study which would be to his advantage. He always imagined himself dressed in fine clothing, and scented fragrance that linger behind, when he leaves a room. Being on the farm would not offer him that prospect. However, being at the mission would prevent him from the exposure to street life and sleeping outdoors. He just needed to get accustomed to sleeping on a bed.

Lily was proud of his decision, though she believed that he would have done well under the influence of Dave and her dad. Not- with standing, she made the appointment and he was ready to go. He didn't have anything to pack, therefore Lily had to take him shopping. Then she took him to the bus stop and saw that he got on the bus to go to the west side of the island, miles away from his familiar stamping ground. "The change of environment will be good for him Lily said." Alphonzo was now in unfamiliar territory. He had to follow routine. He had to go to bed at a certain time. Lights out had to be obeyed. Then the experience at the first overnight mission came back to haunt him. He had to wake at rise and shine. This time it was different. He had to go to the cafeteria for devotion. They sing songs, read the bible and pray before he and twenty-three others did morning duty.

This alternative lifestyle was strange to Alphonzo at first. However, gradually he got accustomed to it and was adjusting to the mission's way of life. One day he found himself doing something he had never done for years. That is, he was writing a letter to Lily. He thanked her for intervening in his life, and that he was adjusting to the conditions beautifully. He was studding but he found it hard to concentrate. However, he remembered her words of encouragement. "You have greatness in you." When she read the letter, she was fully persuaded that together they had made the right decision. For this, she felt a warm glow all over her body. She looked down the road to the future and she saw the business Sign erected on a shop, "Alphonzo's Auto Mechanics." She saw him in his overalls and heard the loud vibration of machines. She smelled the burning of oil and the grease as purposeful work took place.

Next, on Lily's agenda was to liaison with the Manager of the Children's service to improve conditions in that department. What Lily discovered was that, it was a lack of sufficient time that prevented them from imputing the information in the computer. It took longer than they anticipated. Thus, they improved the efficiency of the system by recruiting qualified workers. Henceforth, remuneration and promotion of workers who worked for basic salary for many years, would be taken care of. Not only that, but there would be organized workshops and seminars for training leaders in supervisory positions. This would most likely prevent the catastrophe that caused Tina's life.

Lily imagined herself walking in the building and seeing young efficient' businesslike and committed young people, catering for voiceless children. She could see parents and visitors sitting in padded seats. She could hear the automated system as it summoned clients to different windows to have their business addressed. She saw a clear vision, of labels on glass doors and windows, that instructed and clarified questions of clients, in Spanish, French and English, as people sat comfortably waiting. She smelt the coffee pot on the counter with fresh brewed coffee and saw clients sipping and munching on Graham crackers. Life in the day of a visitor to the department was much different now.

Overcrowded situation caused undue inconvenience through shortness of facilities. A long wait time and increase man hours to accomplish task, that could take a fraction of the time was addressed. She suggested an assessment of the residency, situation. Children who were of certain age, could move on to other institutions for older ones. Also, those whose family situation changed and improved, could move back home. Those who could move back home would certainly create space for others who were waiting to enter.

The matter of failed leadership was also addressed. If effective leadership was in place, perhaps Tina might not have lost her life. Therefore, these charges were pending. Similarly, it was clear that an investigation as to who was responsible for not handling her case more urgently, was most essential. Not for punishing the individual but to understand the inner workings of the system. This would reveal the thought process and organizational skills employed in making such decisions. This travesty of just of how child abuse is handled had to be brought to light. Hence, she made an appointment to see the leadership of the Children's Services to address all these concerns.

This time she didn't choose town hall style meetings but a face to face session, with the leadership. She understood that she was only making the proposals. The leadership had to take them to the Minister of government that handles Children's Affairs. Part of her recommendation was to classify workers in various levels, which would address the disparity of remuneration. There should be six categories. Levels one to six. For example, level One employee would be one who has no formal qualifications but is able to perform work within the scope of this basic level. The employee would be directly supervised in an environment that caters to team spirit and would be given regular on-the job training. Level six on the other hand, would be a director who has achieved relevant, proven documentary evidence or a level three or four Early Childhood Education, or an advanced diploma in Children's Services. She would also receive a diploma in out of hours' care work or such qualification that was deemed worthy of the director of Children's Services. Directors would be categorized in three groups.

Each category had a leader, which would be distinguished by the number of children that fell under his or her leadership. Level one would have 39 students, level 2 40 -59 and Level three 60 clients. This person would be among other things, be responsible for the administration and management of the services, such as its day-to-day operation, recruitment and staffing. Then, workers would be compensated for bringing extra qualification, skill and talent that could make the department more vibrant and productive. For example, if you are a teacher, a nurse, or a highly-qualified clerical personnel, you would be paid extra for the service you could offer. Teachers, nurses and social workers were in demand and several made the Children's Service a career path.

As a result, the institution was upgraded to a 21st century efficient organization. New buildings were erected to reduce the overcrowded situation. When parents go to visit, they never had to wait on the outside. The system was computerized so that at the touch of a button information was found. Where as in the past, people had to wait the whole day to get assistance, their assistance was delivered in less than ten minutes. Not only that, but the institution was given a 5 Star rating.

Lily was on her way to success. She knew how to mix with those at the top of the cooperate world, yet she never lost touch with the common folks. Her purpose was fixed on her chosen pathway to speak for the voiceless. For this reason, she never missed an opportunity to mingle and help them like she did Alphonzo and his step mother. Mother was crippled, almost blind and lived alone. It was only a true test of her resilience, and unfailing spirit of duty, before dishonor, why she sought to help these two people. The old lady was institutionalized in one of the best nursing homes. Some might say you cannot be successful when you spend time with a so called, loser like Alphonzo.

However, prioritizing your time and diligence are key components of success. You must love selflessly. You cannot love unselfishly without employing time, talent and treasure. By helping the least one of these, you do it unto Me, the scripture says. If every successful person in life was to help one homeless and destitute person, rediscover or reinvent themselves, think of how nicer the world would have been.

Some would dare to tell her that she couldn't reach her destiny, if she wasted time on distractions. However, she told them that helping people whether as a facilitator who advocates for changes in the Children Service was worth it. She drew reference from the exposure of over 7000 children who were sexually abused and the investigation of Dioxin poison. She followed lead after lead, until finally the perpetrators were brought to justice. These all came about because of her deliberate choice. This is the choice every effective advocate must make. To her, this was exhilarating, and interesting. They were building blocks of success in the work she was called to do. Spending time with the common folks helped her to see herself in them. In real life though, success doesn't have to be about achieving a big landmark, it is about helping people gain back their self-respect and dignity one person at a time. That's not to say that landmark   or milestones such as landing a lucrative job with Steve and Steve and big promotion that followed were not important; but satisfying the desires of her heart by fulfilling her mother's differed dream for voiceless people and in the process helping others to help themselves was reward that was incomparable.

Chapter 12

Consequently, she was not only effective in the corporate world, her persona gave her a special voice and visibility in the market place of ideas. It wasn't a case of self-promotion or doing things   to be noticed but being popular emerged from the work she did every day to everyday people. Therefore, people took notice of her. She was often featured in the news, on the front page of popular newspapers, and she was a big Social Media fan. One of her closest admirers was those from her Alma mater. So, much so, that she was invited to make the commence address for the graduating class that year. That remarkable success gave butterflies in her stomach for days. Fortunately, she was given a topic that she could use her own experiences to great advantage.

She commenced her address by reading a poem from the Author's collection called: Diamonds in The Rough

Diamonds in The Rough

Just beyond human's approval, lurks
The precious salvage of heaven's joy,
I see them as diamonds in the rough,
Chosen from the unexplained,
They are rugged, coarse, and unkempt –
Paupers, thugs and daring thieves,
Though camouflage by man's perception,
Classified, labeled and ready rejected.
Yet they await their balmy sunburst:
Rescued by God's redemptive plan,
The plan that changes rags for riches;
That transforms man from sin to grace
They move from nothingness to notoriety
By the power of the spoken word.

The Author

These diamonds in the rough, represent the lives of people across all age and spectrum, from children to adults, from main street to Wall Street and from Timbuctoo the big apple. They have fallen through the cracks of irresponsible society. They were mold and shaped by heartless cruelty, some deliberately and others unwittingly. These unfortunate issues emerge from societal failure, that fostered bitterness and selfish abuses by the haves and the privileged. Unfortunately, many were abused by their own peers, because they may be stronger or have a brief advantage. Society wrote them off, before they got a fair chance at life. Some have been given fair chance but made a shipwreck of their lives. If only the society could see them as diamonds in the rough; If only they could be sought and garnered, polish and preserved and give them the tools to reinvent themselves, the world would be so much nicer to rub shoulder with them in the marketplace of life.

She presented the story of Tina as reference. She learned from checking her records at the basic and elementary school levels, that she was as promising as most of the other students. Yet she was abused, neglected to a specimen for experiment that cost only one miserly hundred dollars. Her life was snuffed out by the hand of cruel selfish adults like a pig slaughtered at the butcher's stall. Lily bemoaned the inefficiency of the Children's Service for allowing her to be neglected and killed. She spoke of the courage of her grandmother who in the face of destitution, difficulties and danger, survived under harsh conditions on a bread and butter pension check.

Then she used Alphonzo as her object lesson. She rescued him from the gutters of rejection, hopelessness, failure and of nothingness and instilled in him hope. This allowed him to reinvent himself. He was brought from the gutters of a pauper to the princely palace of self-employment. She gave him a chance to reformation his character by challenging him with work ethics, diligence and the discipline of study. She told of the choices she gave him and his willingness to go to the Rescue Mission, where he pursued the General Education Diploma; graduated and worked as a supervisor for a huge German Automotive and Mechanical Company. This was success. For this, she received a thunderous applause and a standing ovation. She also told of his ambition to manage his own business. Then she dared the audience to take a walk with her. Can you see the sign: "Alphonzo's Automotive? Can you see him proudly dressed in overalls over his shirt and tie? Can you smell the burning of rubber, the grease and engine fluid? Can you hear the crunching of metal and the smooth turning of wheels as industrious workers apply their skills? Can you see him featured on front page of Society's Bill board or The Sunday Gleaner: "From rags to riches." Isn't this, indeed the future of those who dare to dream? That is what success looks like.

Then she went in to the heart of her message. Graduates I speak to you not as one who has no life experience; For God didn't give me the Spirit of timidity but one of power, love, and self-discipline. (Timothy 1:7). She mounted the insignia of her Lily now carved in Gold, under the name of her organization "Voice of the Voiceless." She told her mother's story and the story of the Lily and how the two merged to shape her destiny. She related the success in shaping the Children's Services, and its receiving, a 5 Star rating. Therefore, she justified her calling. When she sat with Alphonzo at an all-night restaurant she was criticized for hanging out with a bomb. Yet, for this cause, she was called, for this cause, she lived.

Then, to you graduates, if you want to be successful you cannot make money be your first choice. (Henry Ford knew better than that when he said a business that makes nothing, but money is a poor business). She couldn't agree more. She related the story of her Dad who was relegated to being label as living a life of nepotism, all because one participant in a companion, couldn't perform as well as his daughter, and wouldn't win the prize money. He was a cheater, because he gave unfair advantage to his daughter. Therefore, he withdrew her from the competition. She also told of a huge company which had to close operation because they were a,' for profit organization" which, gave grudgingly to the public, kept raising prices especially during time of hardship and austerity. Finally, they had to file for bankruptcy. Therefore, the love of money is the root of all evil. (1 Timothy 6:10, KJV)

Consequently, you need to know that, what is important in life that is a matter of choice. A recent (2017) Gallup poll, "The Atlantic journal, that "well-being rises with income at all levels of income, across the board." In other words, as the title of the article reads, "Yes, Money Does not buy Happiness." (November Volume 2 page 32), What the study revealed, is that, there a "strong correlation" between each nation's real GDP per capita and the sense of "well-being" among those Nations and citizens. The data could just as easily be interpreted the other way around: that happiness creates wealth. What's most likely, though, is that as happiness and wealth are part of a cycle. Each one creating more of the other. Assuming you want to create both wealth and happiness for yourself and those around you, you have two approaches: "wait until you're wealthy to be happy or become happier now and there by create more wealth."

Like me, I found tremendous happiness in helping the now polished diamond Alphonso. When I wake at nights, I wake with the voiceless on my mind. There would be the call from the teenage girl, whose mother locked her out for coming home too late and the school boy who had to fight off his wood-be attacker who tried to rape him. Then there was the infant child whose mother beat her for peeing her pants. I have become wealthy in Spiritually, morally and of course I am not the worse off financially. It was rare occasion when I wasn't given a solution to take care of the issues those unfortunates present.

I say issues because they were never problems. I choose the latter above, not to say that I'm wealthy by any stretch of the imagination according visible standards, but I'm wealthy because I have chosen to advocate for the underprivileged which makes me extremely happy, for helping the least of one of these. Happiness is wealth unmatched in physical value.

As a result, I must agree with the author who writes that "Time and money spent on helping a man to better himself is better than doling out cash to him." The author went on to quote the Chinese proverbs that: "If you teach a man to fish, he will always have fish, but if you continue giving him fish, he will remain dependent." I can't help but use Alphonso's success story as example. Many Priests and Levites passed his way and didn't stop. How many politicians have passed on the other side and left him as the man who our Lord illustrated in the story of the Good Samaritan in St, Luke10:25-37. Yet, if it was not for the Good Samaritan who traversed the street, he would have been on the street of no return. She spoke with such passion that it brought applause from the crowd and gave her time to compose herself.

In closing, I would like to draw your attention to the article from Dan Schnabel, (2007) CONTRIBUTION IN THE FORBES MAGAZINE: I've spoken to over 1,200 CEOs, celebrities, authors, politicians and even an astronaut. When speaking to these individuals, I always notice common traits that they all exhibit, which lend to their success. I've captured all these, into the top 14 things that all of them have in common. (December 17,2013) If you can think of any additional ones, leave them in my mailbox. However, I leave you with three.

Firstly, he said successful people know when to stay and when to leave their employment. Successful people know exactly when they should change employers, start a company or fold it. They have good intuition and aren't afraid to make hard choices, despite opposing forces. I would like to expand on one aspect of this quote. That is, to get your promise that you will only keep a nine –to- five job, as a stepping- stone to your own business. Unless of course, you see where you can chart a path to a successful executive, or there is a definite road map to success within the company.

A nine-to-five job is like paying rent. Every month's rent could be the mortgage on your own house. In a nine -to -five- job you collect a pay check every forth night or monthly. When you get promoted; it comes with a cost. The draw -back is that you cannot leave a legacy for your family. When you retire you leave the job behind. You are discarded given a pension without benefits. I can tell you the story of a young man who was a teacher who was employed to one of the better schools in his country, he was promoted to a supervisory position. Yet he yearned for the opportunity to run his own business. However, he saw no prospect, that he couldn't achieve his dream on his nine-to- five job. He migrated, though under dubious circumstances but he was determined to open his own business. Every month he would buy a tool and store it. He eventually opened his own business and did very well. He is on his way to be very rich. Yet it came with the cost of migrating and leaving everything he had behind.

Secondly, successful people do more than what's asked of them. They view their job descriptions as just the beginning of what they can do with their job. After they've completed their mandatory tasks, they will always ask to take on more projects that challenge them. They are even willing to take on the tedious work that no one else wants to do, in order, to be a team player. Henry Ford writes that "Enthusiasm is the yeast that makes your hopes shine to the stars. Enthusiasm is the sparkle in your eyes, the swing in your gait- the grip of your hand, the irresistible surge of will and energy to execute your ideas." Martin Luther King, Jr. would concur when he wrote:"

"If a man is called to be a street sweeper, he should sweep streets even as a Michael Angelo painted, or Beethoven composed music or Shakespeare wrote poetry. He should sweep streets so well that all the hosts of heaven and earth will pause to say, 'Here lived a great street sweeper who did his job well."

Thirdly successful people are willing to fail in order, to eventually succeed. All successful people know that it doesn't come easy and they are bound to fail more than they will succeed at anything. They are willing to learn from each failure, as it will help them make better decisions that lead to success later. While many people give up after failing at something, a successful person will persevere. If he didn't fail, Thomas Edison might not have become America's most well- known and prolific innovator. Like most entrepreneurs, when Edison first started his career, he was certain he had observed a fundamental problem he could solve. Specifically, Edison noticed that whenever Congress voted on an issue, each senator would stand one by one and call out his vote. To Edison, the inefficiency of such a system was an absolute disaster, and he realized that he could invent a system to quickly tally all the votes and skip the unnecessary and wasteful step of calling out votes. That resulted in the light bulb. He also created such great innovations as photographing. He was a savvy businessman, he held more than 1,000 patents for his inventions. In his words "Many of life's failures are people who did not realize how close they were to success when they gave up.

Thomas Edison's shows Innovativeness, and grit. Gritty action has the tendency to sustain interest in, and effort toward very long- term goal. No one can deny the fact that Edison was a man of grit. He operated in what came to light, posted January 2014 that he was performing them in the 21 Century, yet he lived in the nineteenth century. Well psychology is just catching up with him, just like the words of the man who says: The first requisite for success is to develop the ability to focus and apply your mental and physical energies to the problem at hand - without growing weary. As Thomas Edison puts it: "I didn't fail 1000 times. The light bulb was an invention with 1000 steps." Because such thinking is often difficult, there seems to be no limit to which some people will go to avoid the effort and labour that is associated with it.

Consequently, I leave you this evening and I hope you feel a sense of pride that one so young, trained at your University could be called upon to give the commence address. This means that you are in good hands and you are ready for the Market p lace. You will be masters of your own destiny. Some of you will chart your course in unknown territory, where hardship is your constant companion because of the choices you have made. However, remember you are not alone nor are you the first. When you contemplate giving up, remember Rosa Parks daring quest. When you think of giving up remember, Fidel Castro who was undaunted, unloved by Americans, but ruled as a revolutionary because they couldn't beat him at his game. When you feel like giving up remember Martin Luther, Mahatma Gandhi and our supreme example the Lord Jesus Christ. Therefore, as I have started with a poem, I will close with an excerpt of another poem. It was originally called "The Gate of the Year" "then retitled Safer than a known way"

I said to the man who stood at the gate of the year.

'Give me a light that I may tread safely into the unknown.'

And he replied,

Go into the darkness and put your hand into the hand of God that shall be to you better than light and safer than a known way.

The audience responded with a thunderous applause, which went on for too long. At the end of the commencement Lily had the Doctor of Laws degree conferred upon her. She came as Lily Abigail Shelly- Smith Parks and when she retrieved her steps she was Dr. Lily Abigail Shelly Smith Parks. Then it was time for signing autographs and receiving congratulations. People, especially the graduates lined up for signing. She spent a good twenty-five minutes rushing through her signing because she was invited to have brunch with the faculty. To her fondest memory and great surprise, she saw Raoul sitting proudly with the faculty, robed in his Doctorate PhD Academic Regalia. She was impressed by his progress and demeanour. He now had an academic PhD while she had Dr. of laws conferred upon her, not that she was not capable and ambitious, but she spent her time caring for the less fortunate. Therefore, she went across the room to congratulate him. He didn't entertain much conversation with her because he vowed to turn the tides on her and play hard to get. He just shoved a book in her hand and made an early departure. From all account he carried out his threat. She played a game of hard to get in college and now it was his turn.

Chapter 13

She went home with butterflies in her stomach. She set up the whole night reading his vision. He was no longer a leader of history driven by his past. He was a leader of destiny. He asked the pertinent question with a sense of audacious hope. The sense of reality she doggedly escaped had now changed course. She will, now become the pursuer and he will become the object of her passion. So, with much pride he set his vision assail. Consequently, he boldly asked himself the incredulous question, what does destiny look like in my future? Have I got the fortitude and tenacity to conquer this giant? Will I have her bowing at my knees? Hence, let me by the powers that be, embark on this noble path of reinventing myself. He realized that potential wasn't enough, he had to proactively define destiny which began as a photograph in his heart where it mushroomed to expectation and hope. He saw in his mind's eye what this Proverbs 31st woman, Lily was earnestly a spiritual knockout.

Consequently, he skillfully captured it in a book "Destiny delayed puts the future in perspective." He expected Lily to spend a few days reading and pondering over what he considered his master piece, the deep thoughts of his brilliant mind. But it showed that he didn't know the woman he was attempting to woo. She was a go getter, non- nonsense single woman who had risen to the top of her corporate world, though, not in academics but she arrived on the doorsteps of hard knocks. She boldly, opened the door and announced herself to the world as a woman of purpose. She was totally aware of the hardships of life of voiceless folks and the immutable role she had to play as a woman. So, she wasn't a woman who court fear, she knew her self- esteem. She didn't need anyone's endorsement for her to be noticed. She doesn't allow anything stand in her way. Thus, a one fifty-page book was no match for her intellect. Arguably though, when she called early next morning before he went to work, he just couldn't believe that she would sit up to read and digested its contents of the book. So, he ignored her phone call. She could by no means calling to say she had finished.

Consequently, she didn't have breakfast but presented herself at the staff dining room to meet him. And true to form he had breakfast with her but couldn't entertain any conversation, except for mere formalities. His lecture would end two and a half hours' time because he had back to back classes. She called her office and set her staff to work and went to the library to occupy her time. She browsed through several periodicals as if she was looking for specific information and as the hour came she left in a flash to meet him at his classroom door. However, as it turned out, Mr. Hard-to-get left five minutes earlier because he had a business interruption at his office and so he had a valid apology. This he thoroughly enjoyed. He laughed all the way to his office.

However, Lily understood; she didn't take no for an answer. Therefore, she used one of her friend's cell phone, and called him. Before he could answer she blurted out "Professor you must love with your heart, not with your brains, and not the gentleman you have anywhere else." Brains can certainly think but heart was made for love. As far as I am concerned you make a lousy lover. Before he could respond she hung up the phone. This tossed the professor in a tailspin to redeem himself without being ill mannered, unkind nor fearful.

This reversed all his attempt of hard to get right back in his face. This hurt his pride and demeaned his manhood. Henceforth, Mr. Professor Raoul set out to recapture some respectability and self -image. He didn't disguise behind a childish teenager using the other's phone to call but being the man who thinks quickly on his feet, he improved on her method, so he devised a master plan. He called Jerry, introduced himself and he was elated to get his response. He thought that he would be totally missing from her life. Therefore, he asked pertinent questions of her dad. He inquired about favourite food, colour and make plans to turn her mysterious world upside down. First with total confidence and a touch of mystery, he purchased an oversize bouquet of white lilies and drove to her office gaudily dressed, to make his presentation. He thought for a moment that he was bordering on the ridiculous and would make himself look foolish. However, he single- headedly braced himself for any reply she chose. He approached her with a tape recorder playing one of her mother's favourite tune.

(This Magic Moment. By Jay and the Americans)

This magic moment
so different and so new
Was like any other
until I kissed you,
And then it happened
It took me by surprise
I knew that you felt it too
by the look in your eyes,
It's sweeter than wine

This was certainly sweeter, much sweeter, than the vintage wine from the dark red grapes. She was completely blown away. When he knocked at her door she didn't have the slightest idea that he would come looking for her. Her friends found it convenient to excuses themselves. She was speechless. She was now at his mercy, at the receiving end, unable to make her usually bold speech. She literally trembled and stuttered in his presence. He was totally transformed from professor to a lover and regular man who was courteous, gracious and oozed a special sophisticated charm. He was nothing short of a miracle. Such debonair qualities moved her and surpass her expectation. To make matters even more romantic, he placed a kiss on her lips ever so gently with such warmth and gracious invitation. She closed her eyes and half opened her mouth as if she was waiting for another. Then he took her in his arms and danced to the magic in the moment. He clapped his hands lightly as if to call her back to earth. Without asking, he took up the bouquet of flowers, lead and she flowed him. He took her to her favourite restaurant where a pianist was playing "This magic moment." She was certainly taken by surprise. And the rest is history. Their first children were twins whom they named Jeremiah and Zelda Romans Parks.

www.ingramcontent.com/pod-product-compliance
Lightning Source LLC
Chambersburg PA
CBHW051449130726
47987CB00005B/2251